FIFTY SHADES OF SNOW

Lock Down Publications and Ca$h

Presents

Fifty Shades of Snow
A Novel by **A. Roy Milligan**

Lock Down Publications
Po Box 944
Stockbridge, Ga 30281

Visit our website @
www.lockdownpublications.com

Copyright by A. Roy Milligan
Fifty Shades of Snow

All rights reserved. No part of this book may be reproduced in any form or by electronic or mechanical means, including information storage and retrieval systems without permission in writing from the publisher, except by a reviewer who may quote brief passages in review.

First Edition

Printed in the United States of America

This is a work of fiction. Names, characters, places, and incidents either are products of the author's imagination or are used fictitiously. Any similarity to actual events or locales or persons, living or dead, is entirely coincidental.

Lock Down Publications
Like our page on Facebook: Lock Down Publications @
www.facebook.com/lockdownpublications.ldp

Stay Connected with Us!

Text **LOCKDOWN** to 22828 to stay up-to-date with new releases, sneak peaks, contests and more…

Thank you.

Submission Guideline.

Submit the first three chapters of your completed manuscript to ldpsubmissions@gmail.com, subject line: Your book's title. The manuscript must be in a .doc file and sent as an attachment. Document should be in Times New Roman, double spaced and in size 12 font. Also, provide your synopsis and full contact information. If sending multiple submissions, they must each be in a separate email.

Have a story but no way to send it electronically? You can still submit to LDP/Ca$h Presents. Send in the first three chapters, written or typed, of your completed manuscript to:

LDP: Submissions Dept
Po Box 944
Stockbridge, Ga 30281

DO NOT send original manuscript. Must be a duplicate.

Provide your synopsis and a cover letter containing your full contact information.

Thanks for considering LDP and Ca$h Presents.

CHAPTER
ONE

Steve was on his way home from work a few hours earlier than usual. The coronavirus pandemic had caused a material shortage, which was causing a lot of problems at his job. Everything was arriving slowly, and much of what they needed was on backorder. It was frustrating because the lack of hours was making Steve's checks get shorter and shorter.

It was early in the afternoon, so the traffic was light, making the drive home much less stressful than usual. Still, he didn't know what he was going to do to make up for his recently declining income. He was wanting to work more hours, but they weren't available. He was going to have to do something, but didn't want to think about it, so he turned up the radio. Lil Baby's newest hit was on, and he hummed along. He tried to call his girlfriend Angelia a few times, but she didn't answer. He was trying to figure out if she was hungry or not, but he assumed she was asleep.

Steve pulled onto his street, and saw a few of the neighborhood kids riding around on bikes. Some of the high school kids were playing basketball at the park. As he approached his house, he saw an 86' Monte Carlo parked in the driveway on some 24" rims. He pulled up in the driveway and parked next to the car, wondering if he had ever seen it before. He picked up his phone and tried to call Angelia again as he got out of the car. Still no answer, so he walked up to the door and unlocked it. When he opened it and stepped inside, he heard, "Yes, baby! Fuck me harder!" He paused inside the doorway for a minute then closed the door, and his heart dropped into his stomach. He recognized the voice; it was Angelia.

"What the fu . . . " he started to say, then he sprinted up the stairs, skipping three at a time. When he got to the top of the stairs, he busted straight through the slightly opened door. "What the fuck are you doing?" Steve yelled, feeling a rush of anger as he saw some unfamiliar guy pounding Angelia from behind.

"Oh, my God! Get out!" Angelia screamed. Although her face was already flushed from the sex, it immediately got deep red with embarrassment. "What are you doing here?" she yelled as she jumped up and covered her naked body with a fluffy pink blanket.

There was a moment of silence. Steve's hands began to tremble with rage before he said, "The fuck you mean, what am I doing here? This is my house! Who is this nigga?"

"My bad, I ain't know she had a man. I will leave right now," the man said, with both of his hands up, ass naked. He was shocked to see Steve standing there and his erection showed it. His penis went from hard to soft in a matter of seconds while the condom hung off the end of it. He held his hands out to the side and slowly started gathering his things. Steve took two steps toward him with his fist balled up.

"Bro, don't run up on me. I said I'll leave."

Steve thought for a moment about what he said. He could let the guy just leave, but he didn't care about peace right now. He stepped up to him and started swinging, missing the first two punches but landing the third. His punch didn't do enough damage, because before he knew it, he was up in the air, then laying on his back on the hardwood floor being punched in the face.

"Stop! Please stop!" Angelia screamed, pulling the guy off her boyfriend and pushing him out of the bedroom door. "Go, please! Get out!"

"I told your ass, don't run up on me," he yelled before walking down the stairs and out the door.

Angelia walked over to Steve and helped him up. "Are you okay? I'm sorry."

"Let me go," he said as he jerked away from her and held his swollen eye. "Why the fuck do you have a nigga in our house fucking? What is wrong with you?"

"You haven't fucked me in four days. What do you expect?" She rolled her eyes.

"Bitch! Four days? That's all it takes for you to go get fucked? Four days? So, for the last six years, every time it's been four days, you go get fucked, because this is not the only four days it has been. I can't believe this shit, you dirty bitch! Right in our bed too!" Steve was pissed off. This wasn't the first, second, or even third time he caught her cheating, but this was the first time he saw her having sex with another man. His heart was shattered, and he had a knot in his stomach. "Why? Just tell me why, Angelia. Why do you treat me like this? Do you not want to be with me anymore?"

"Yes, I do. I'm sorry. I'm really sorry." She walked towards him while wrapped in her blanket.

"Don't touch me," he said as he stepped back with a disgusted look on his face. "Go get in the shower or something."

Without saying a word, Angelia turned around and walked into the bathroom. She turned on the water and waited for it to warm up. This time she was caught red-handed, and she didn't have any excuse that could come close to making sense. She was agitated as she stood there, speechless. After a minute, she got in the shower, and Steve walked into the bathroom behind her.

"And throw those sheets in the fucking trash!" he yelled, putting both his hands on his head while he looked at himself in the mirror. He walked out of the bathroom, and leaned back against the wall. Tears welled up in his eyes while he slid down the wall to the floor. He put his head in his hands and tried to prevent himself from crying. He was hurt, confused, and had no idea what to do about any of this. He wanted to leave, but he had nowhere comfortable to go. He didn't want to tell his mom what happened, because then she would hate Angelia even more than she already did.

Thoughts came across Steve's mind like a row of cars on the freeway. He couldn't focus. The riot of distressed emotions was hurting him to the depths of his soul. Tears of sadness filled his eyes again, but he got control of himself before they fell. He could not afford to be a crying mess now, his pride would not allow it. He knew that he deserved better.

Though Steve gave it his all, his all was not enough to fight back the flood of tears. Grief and frustration over what he just witnessed consumed his heart, causing a deep injury that no one could see. His tears broke forth like water from a broken dam, trickling down his cheeks. He wondered why this happened, but he didn't know. He was hoping that Angelia would be honest with him and tell him.

He knew that his looks weren't the problem. He had smooth brown skin, and was a handsome 27 year old man that stood 6'2" at about 230 pounds with a nice athletic body. He always took good care of himself, with his hair and mustache lined up to perfection. He was mixed with black and white, and his hair stayed cut low with 6 big waves on his head. All the women loved his hair, and how perfect his waves always looked.

CHAPTER
TWO

Angelia took her time in the bathroom. It was over an hour before she came out, since she was too embarrassed and ashamed to face Steve. When she finally came out, she saw him sitting on the floor against the wall with his head in his lap. She didn't say anything to him. Instead, she just walked over to the bed and laid down.

About five minutes later, he stood up and picked his cell phone up off the floor. "I'll be back," he said quietly as he walked toward the door.

"Where are you going?" she asked softly, but he ignored her and kept walking. He went downstairs, and out the door. He jumped in his car, and called one of his homeboys to tell him that he was going to swing by. The whole way there, his mind kept replaying the scene he had just witnessed over and over. Although he didn't feel like talking about what had happened, he needed a friend. Steve pulled up at James' house, and walked in the side door.

"Damn, nigga! Who whooped your ass?" James asked, laughing while glancing over his shoulder to look at Steve. He kept laughing and went back to playing NBA2K on the PlayStation.

Steve walked into the living room and sat down on the couch next to James. "He ain't whoop my ass. He got a punch or two off."

"Who? Seriously, you were fighting for real?"

"Yeah, man," Steve said as he leaned back on the couch. His phone vibrated, and he saw a text come through from Angelia. He hesitated a second before opening it. Then started going through his phone a couple minutes later, reading the 'I'm sorry' text messages from her. She was writing paragraphs.

Angelia: Baby, I'm so sorry. Please forgive me. There's no excuse for this. I just really felt unwanted by you and thought you had someone else. The last few times we had sex, it seemed like you weren't into it. I love you so much and I don't want us to break up. I just need to feel wanted by you again. Please show me you still want to be with me, that's all I'm asking.

James had stopped playing the game and was looking at Steve curiously. "Nigga, who was you fighting?" he asked.

"Oh . . . this nigga at the gas station. Nigga was talking about, I took his spot or some dumb shit. Hold on," Steve lied as he texted back.

Steve: You know I don't have or want anyone but you. You're acting like you want to be with someone else since you're having these different guys around. I keep catching you talking to and texting with these different dudes, and now I catch you fucking one. That's a slut ass move. Why would a nigga want to be with a girl like that? And how are you feeling unwanted? I do everything for you. Anything you ask, I do. What am I going to do with you? What did I do for you to treat me like this? Do you know how many women would kill to be with a man like me?

He looked at James after sending his text and said, "Yeah, a nigga was tripping. I had to piece the nigga up right fast. He caught me good a couple times though."

"My nigga," James said as he gave him a pound. "Sometimes you definitely have to put paws on niggas out here. He was lucky I wasn't there. He would have been on a stretcher," he said while laughing, but noticed that Steve wasn't laughing with him. He looked sad and sick in the face.

"Bro, you straight?"

Steve shook his head and couldn't control the hurt he felt. "I can't lie to you . . . I just caught a nigga in the house fucking Angelia."

"What!" James' jaw dropped. He was shocked. "In the act?"

"Yeah."

"What happened?"

"I lost it and charged at the nigga."

"Who was the nigga?"

"I don't know, probably a nigga from Detroit. I never seen him or his car before."

"Damn, you seen the car too?"

"Yeah, the nigga was parked right in the driveway when I pulled up, like he lived at the bitch or something. It threw me off when I first pulled up, because usually if it's something sneaky going on, a nigga gone park on the street, down the street, or around the corner. This nigga was in the driveway, bro. Damn near parked right in the middle of it. I was on the grass a little when I pulled up on the side of his shit."

James had slid off his couch, and was on the floor from laughing so hard. "You say . . . this nigga . . . was parked right in the middle like ain't shit wrong. I'm dead!" James said, cracking up so hard that his yellow face was now red as fire.

"Hell yeah! So, I get out the car. For a minute I try to think about who I know with a burgundy 86' Monte Carlo SS on some rims. The motherfucker was cold though, I ain't gone lie. He had that bitch done up right. I was trying to think, so I called her . . . remind you I had been calling the bitch for like 30 minutes straight and she wasn't answering. I got home early because this Covid shit got everything all fucked up. I'm trying to see if this dumb bitch hungry, and she at the crib getting her mutherfucking back blew out," he said, shaking his head.

CHAPTER
THREE

James shook his head and composed himself. He felt bad for Steve. He knew Steve loved Angelia, but he didn't like the type of woman she was or how she'd been treating his friend. "I keep telling you to leave that girl."

"I am this time. This overboard. She had a whole nigga in my house! This bitch ain't helped with a single bill since Covid started, bro."

"I thought she was getting unemployment money?"

"She got $7,000 on back pay and asked me to help her get her body done. Got her a booty and shit like she been wanting."

"I remember, but that was like 8 months ago. She ain't on it no more?"

"Yeah, she is still on it, but she ain't trying to pay anything, bro. I just let her keep that little shit. It be like $500 a week or something."

"Nigga, that can help. Especially with you being behind on your rent. I don't know why you keep trying to take care of that girl when she's a grown woman. How old is she anyway?"

"27, the same as us."

"Fuck that. You need to find another woman that will treat you better. You don't even cheat on that girl or anything. You treat her like a queen, and she out here fucking other dudes in your house."

"I know, right? That's what I'm saying. I told her that shit too."

James laughed. "Told her what?"

"I told her I never cheated on her."

"What did she say?"

"She said that she felt like I had been cheating on her."

James shook his head. "I couldn't be with a girl like that. No way."

Another text came through to Steve's phone from Angelia. As he read through the lengthy text, he nodded his head, disappointed in his girlfriend.

Angelia: Do you know how many guys would kill to be with me? Have you thought about that? I'm a good woman, but any woman that's not feeling loved or needed is going to look elsewhere for what she's missing. I love you and want to be with you, but you need to realize what you have as well. I am very sorry for what happened, and that you had to see that. I promise you that it won't happen again if you just give me one more chance. I'll show you I can be the woman you know I am. Loyal, trustworthy, and determined to make this work.

"So, if you caught your wife with another man in your bed, what would you do?" Steve asked while responding to the text. "Wait, read this before I text her back."

Steve handed his phone to James. "Is this Angelia saying how sorry she is?"

"Yeah."

James took a moment to read through the text, and all he could do was shake his head. "I'm sorry to tell you this, but you deserve way better than her. Way better. First of all, if a real woman has a problem at home . . . and this is just my opinion . . . better yet, this is a fact. If me or my wife has an issue, whether it's one of us feeling unloved or unwanted or whatever, we come to each other to communicate about the issue. We don't invite another soul into our bodies. She's a little girl, bro. I've always told you that. She is supposed to come to you, not fuck another nigga in your bed. She's acting like it's your fault or something too. That shit's stupid, bro."

"What if she did come to me, but I didn't realize it or pay no attention to her?"

"Well shit, I mean that's on you if that's what happened, but it still doesn't give her the right to cheat or have another man inside the house you both live and sleep in. She's going to get someone killed with the way she's acting. Nigga, niggas get killed over that kinda shit. Eboni would never do that, bro. She would leave me before she cheats on me, and I would do the same."

"See, that's what I'm about to explain to her," Steve said as he looked down at his phone and started texting again.

Steve: *I feel like you should have come to me and told me how you felt about everything. I do realize that you are a good woman, but I'm confused about why you treat me like I'm some bum ass nigga out here. I need to think everything through, because this shit hurt me badly. I can't believe what I saw when I walked in.*

"I don't want to judge your situation too much. Obviously, you love this girl. You have been with her for what, 6 or 7 years now?"

"Yeah, something like that."

"So, that's about the same amount of time I've been married to Eboni. I think you need to talk to her, face to face, and not over text because things can easily be misinterpreted that way. And, of course, you should want to look your woman in the eyes when you're pouring your heart out to her, you know? But sit her down and tell her how you feel, then listen to how she feels, then come up with a solution to try to make it work if that's what you both want. Explain to her how someone could have easily been killed today with how that went down. That was a dangerous situation. See, me . . . I woulda shot him and probably shot her ass too. I don't know if I coulda stayed calm after seeing that shit. I can't even imagine Eboni having sex with another man, let alone me walking in on her doing it. I probably would have went crazy. I'm sure she would feel the same way about me doing that shit too."

"See, that's what I want. Y'all got something real. I've always told you that I admire you and Eboni's relationship. I'm taking your advice and going to sit down and talk with her, I think."

"Yeah, try it. It can't hurt. Make sure you don't just blame her, when you're talking to her. Try to see where she is coming from, even though it's going to be hard not to just get mad."

"If you caught Eboni getting banged from the back . . . keep it real . . . would you accept her back? I'm talking, right here on this couch, butt ass naked, another nigga whole dick in her and she screaming."

James laughed. "Shit . . . is his dick bigger than mine?"

"The same size."

"I'm just playing, nigga. No, she's done after some shit like that."

"Well, why are you telling me to talk to her then, because that's exactly what just happened to me."

"Because our situation is different. We are married and have a kid. I mean, you caught niggas in her phone she was texting. You caught her showing her ass on Instagram, well, body pics. You caught her texting niggas, sending pics, and you still ain't leave her. Her fucking a dude is a whole different level, but you seem to still not be done with her, so I'm just trying to be a good nigga and support your feelings, but honestly, I would be done."

CHAPTER
FOUR

That crushed Steve. The pain hit him real deep, and stirred back up his emotions forcefully. He was back to feeling hurt with no appetite even though he hadn't eaten a thing. Soon, his phone vibrated again. It was Angelia calling.

"Hello," he answered.

"You done texting?"

"Naw, I'm not. I was about to text back."

"Can you come home, please?" She started crying. "I'm so sorry, Steve. I swear it won't happen again . . . okay . . . okay, Steve?"

She continued to cry her heart out over the phone. He just held the phone in his hand completely speechless. He was sick inside.

"P . . . please forgive me, okay?" She cried some more. "I will be here whenever you get here. I love you."

"I'll be there in a little bit," he said before hanging up.

"That was Angelia?"

"Yeah, she over there crying and shit, saying sorry," Steve said as he stood up and stretched his arms out.

"What you about to do?"

"Bouta go to the crib and lay down. I need to think."

"You sure you don't want the guest room? I don't want you to snap and beat Angelia's ass over there."

Steve laughed. "Naw, I'm good, bro. I'ma just take a nap at the crib, probably on the couch or something."

"Alright, bro. Call me if you need me."

"Alright, fasho." He walked toward the door, then stopped a few feet from it and paused. He turned around and said, "Aye, do you think me not like being a street nigga, or really getting some money got something to do with Angelia cheating?"

"What you mean?"

"Every nigga I den caught her with, be these flashy dressing ass niggas with nice cars and shit. Like a few niggas in her DM be from Miami. They got boats and shit, nice cars, and all that shit. Another dude she was texting was from Detroit. She used to say he was like a party promoter and she just helped him promote, but she was sending him pussy pics and shit. I checked his Facebook, and he looks like he's getting money too. I mean, I work a 9-5, $18 an hour job, and grab a couple ounces of cocaine every few weeks. The guys she talking to getting it. Even the dude today, the nigga car was done up. I knew it wasn't a nigga in Pontiac. Not saying us Pontiac niggas don't be coming out nice, but this mutherfucker was cold. Then, this nigga had so much ice around his neck like he was a rapper or something. I was just thinking about all that shit. Does that make sense to you?"

"If that's what she's really about and looking for, she don't deserve you."

"Naw, I don't think that. I'm asking you like if I was balling, do you think she would still cheat?"

"That's not what a relationship is based on or should be based on. My wife would have the same respect for me whether I had money or not. I mean, you can't only respect your partner if they got money, and cheat on them if they don't. That shit ain't right. Do you feel like she thinks you a bum or something?"

"Not really. I mean she has thrown these niggas in my face in the past, like just talking about a dude's car. I've seen text messages with her and her friends talking about dudes with certain cars and shit. I don't know."

James laughed. "Bro, stay out of that woman's phone, please!"

Steve laughed, gave James a nod, then walked out the door. "I'll figure it out."

He drove home, taking the long way so he could have more time to clear his mind. When he got close, he decided to stop and get some gas, even though he didn't need any.

Steve parked his Impala at the pump, got out, and went inside. He approached the counter and said, "Let me get $5 on pump three," as he slid a $5 bill across the counter. The employee took it and nodded without saying a word. He turned around and started walking toward the door, and suddenly he saw a light skinned girl smiling as she came through the door.

"Hey, Steve."

"Hey, hey. How you doing, Shila?"

"Good, and yourself?"

"I'm good." He gave her a smile and continued, "Well, it's good seeing you."

"Dang! I couldn't even get a hug?" she said, throwing her hands up while smiling at him.

He laughed, and gave her a one-sided arm hug. "Oh, and your number," Shila said, giving him a sexy look.

"You know I can't do that. I got a girlfriend."

"Oh, I forgot. Angelia, right? Ahaa! That's funny!" She started cracking up and shaking her head. "Well, let me know when you ready for a loyal woman."

"What's that supposed to mean? My girl is loyal. That's what's wrong with y'all Pontiac chicks. You always trying to break up a happy home."

"Nigga, please. Gone with your soft ass, Steve, for I break your heart right in this gas station." She turned around and walked away. "A bitch like me wouldn't give a nigga like you a real chance anyway," she said under her breath.

CHAPTER
FIVE

Steve shook his head and walked to his car. He pulled out the handle to the gas pump and started to fill his tank. When he looked up, he saw Shila pull up next to him in her Benz SUV with her windows down. "Damn, you still in that old ass Impala? What's that a 2005?" The five friends inside her SUV all started laughing.

"You was the one just asking for my number though."

"Oh, I was just on some getting back shit. Don't even THINK I was serious!" she said, as she pulled away laughing. He heard one of the girls in the back say something about him only putting five dollars in his tank. He laughed and shook his head as he hung up the pump.

"At least mine is paid for," he said to himself as he got in and started his car.

He was in deep thought as he drove away. He didn't need more bullshit on top of what already happened earlier. He called James to keep his mind in check.

"What's up, bro?" he answered.

"Nothing much, just leaving the gas station. Why Shila and some of her homegirls just try to stunt on me, talking about what year is my car?"

"Damn, for real? What's her problem?"

"She was mad I ain't give her my number."

"Man, fuck her and her sack chasing ass friends. They all bag chasers. They tryna fuck the nigga with the biggest bag out there. I wouldn't hit any of of them with your dick, nigga."

They both laughed.

"For real, KP, Stan, and all them niggas be fucking all them little hoes," James said.

"Oh, yeah? Did you get KP's number? I'm thinking about hollering at them boys to see what they got going on."

"You already know what they got going on. They got a nice bag. Them boys got Porsches, Maseratis, Ranges, and all kinds of shit over there. I got KP's number, hold on. Damn, I don't see it. Just pull up on him. They be right on the block all day long. You will see him out there."

"Yeah, I'm about to ride down on him and see what he's talking about."

"Okay, bet. Tell him I said what up. Be safe over there. I'm sure the Feds watching all them niggas over that way."

"Damn, don't say that," Steve replied.

They laughed.

"I'm just being real, bro. If they ain't talking about shit you want to hear, holla at my cousin Juice. He in that lane heavy too. I'm bouta text you his number."

"Oh yeah, Juice my nigga too. I ain't seen that nigga in a minute. Good looking."

"Fasho."

"Alright, bro."

Steve hung up the phone and drove over to KP's block. As he pulled up, he saw that James was right; there were foreign cars lined up on both sides of the street and people were everywhere. After looking around while driving slow, he was able to spot KP standing by his white Porsche with his shirt off. "What's up, nigga?"

"What up doe, my nigga?" KP replied.

Steve came to a stop next to KP. "Chillin. Just seeing if I could holla at you about something real quick."

"Hell yeah, park right there and get out. Aye, y'all move out the way! Let him park right there for a second," he said to a group of girls that were standing around in front of his car.

Steve parked, stepped out, and embraced KP with open arms. "How you been? This your shit? This bitch right here is cold-blooded."

"Yeah, I just copped this one not too long ago. I been cooling. Tryna stay out these hating ass niggas way, you feel me?"

"Hell yeah, same here. You still be fucking with the white?"

"Yes, sir. What you trying to get?"

"I just be grabbing like two ounces. How much do you charge for that?"

"$1,500, and you gone get 28 grams back if you drop it in the water. It's all there. I ain't playing games with it. What you been paying?"

"Shit, like $1,200 for real, and it's all there."

"Shit, that's a sweet price, homie. I could probably do $1,400 if you grabbing two. Yeah, $1,400 I can do for you."

"I might have to check it out. What's your number?" Steve handed KP his phone, and he put his number in it.

"Fuck with me, bro. I'll throw you more on top of those two if you fuck with me. I got them bitches. Look," KP said as he popped his trunk. Steve looked in the trunk, and KP unzipped a duffle bag with 8 kilos of cocaine in it.

"Damn, nigga! You ain't fucking around."

"You damn right. Fuck with me. Lock that number in. You still be messing with that lil' bad chick you been with for years? Angelia?"

Steve laughed. "Yeah, that's still my baby. She's in trouble right now though."

"Shit, you know these hoes out here getting active," KP said, laughing and shaking his head. He was in that circle where he knew who the real money getters were in Pontiac and Detroit. That made him know things about Angelia that even Steve didn't. "Holla at me though. Let me take this call," KP said as he walked away on his phone.

CHAPTER SIX

Steve got in his car and called Juice, and they met up at a park on the east side of Pontiac. It was crowded out on this sunny day, but he noticed Juice standing off to the side in a yard. Juice gave Steve a nod when they met eyes.

"Just jump in," Steve told him as he sat back down in his car.

"What's up, my nigga? Where your ass been?" Juice asked, smiling while shutting the door. "Bro called me and told me you wanted to holla at me. I'm like, I ain't seen that nigga in years. You been good out here?"

Steve laughed. "Yeah, I been cooling. I be working damn near every day, so I be staying out the way."

"Oh, you still be doing your thing though?"

"Hell yeah, what the ounces of white going for right now?"

"Ouu, you don't want to hear the prices right now . . . they like $1,700 at the moment. These niggas be playing games out here so much, so you gotta be aware. I'ma keep it real with you because you family. It's all there."

"Damn, that's high. I just pulled up on KP. He told me $1,500, and I'll get 28 grams back if I cook it."

Juice laughed and shook his head. "Yeah, that's what he says until you buy that shit. Naw, his straight though. He be remixing, but he got a good cut, so when you cook it, it all still comes back. This shit I got doe, it's that flake for real." Juice pulled out a half ounce from his pocket and opened it. "Look at this shit." He broke open the chunk for Steve to see.

"Yeah, that shit is flaky as hell. And damn, that shit strong smelling too."

"Yeah, this is the shit, I'm telling you."

"I'ma have to fuck with you. That shit looks good. The shit I've been getting doesn't look like that. I pay $1,200."

Juice laughed. "Nigga, $1,200? I know damn well it ain't this. If it is, I need to be buying from you."

They both laughed.

"Nigga, for real. If I was you, I would not buy from none of these niggas around here. You got a Mexican chick. You better find out where her people at. You playing."

Steve laughed.

"No, I'm serious, bro. She the plug. You got to work your hand before another nigga work his hand on her. I be hearing her name ringing. I know she taking you down through there."

"Taking me down through there? Her name ringing? What you saying?"

Juice squeezed his lips together as if he already may have said too much.

"She be fucking with Esha. Nigga, all Esha do is fuck with niggas from the city with money. It's a few niggas around here I done heard your girl was dealing with, including the nigga you said you just left."

"KP?"

"Yeah, him and one of his homeboys."

"KP's fat, black ass? You sure you talking bout my girl?"

"Yes, your girl. Short, long hair, kinda looks like a Mexican version of Kim Kardashian. Her name Angie, Angela, or something, right?"

"Angelia, yeah."

"Yeah, bro. She be creeping around this bitch. You ain't been around mingling much or you woulda fasho heard some shit. I ain't seen you in like 2-3 years, nigga. How I damn near know your girl's name? So you know I ain't lying!"

"That's crazy," Steve said, sliding down in his seat. He couldn't believe what he was hearing. "I'ma have to leave her ass alone."

"Before you do, get a plug," Juice said, laughing. Steve looked at Juice and realized that he had no idea how bad he was hurt right now, so he laughed with him.

"How would you go about that?" Steve asked.

"Shit, just ask her about her family and where they at. Tell her you trying to get a plug, fuck it." Juice laughed. "You ain't as dark as me, so them Mexicans will fuck with you. My dark ass . . . they gone be like, naw, nigga."

They both laughed.

"You silly as hell. I'ma see what I can do."

"And when you get them, make sure you holla at me."

"Fasho. Alright, let me get to the crib. I'll holla at you. Lock my number in."

"I got you. Be safe out here," Juice said as he got out of the car.

CHAPTER
SEVEN

Steve drove away, heading home. While Steve drove, he was deep in his thoughts. It was like the closer he got to home, the sadder he became. He felt his anger rise up to the surface again, and he wasn't ready to head back to the crib just yet, so he slowed down a bit and hit extra corners. The vision of his girl being fucked by another man kept replaying over and over in his head. Part of him couldn't believe it. Part of him knew it was true. Then the anxiety set in, followed by the rage. He shook his head trying to banish the thoughts of her from his mind. He didn't care about anything anymore, but at the same time he did. Before he knew it, his eyes welled up. He blinked, and streams of tears rolled down his cheeks faster than his heartbeat.

"Fuck! God, please help me out," Steve prayed. "I need you right now. I love this girl, and I don't know what to do. Should I scream at her or hug her, and tell her I love her? Please, God, help me. Guide me about what I should say, how I should act, and where I should sleep."

As he pulled up in the driveway, it was a bit early still, but he was hoping she was already asleep. So much was on his mind.

When he put his key in the door, he could smell the food being cooked inside. He walked in and saw Angelia and her friend Tasha cooking in the kitchen. The food smelled good, and Steve was hungry. He already knew he was too mad to eat though.

"Hey, Steve," Tasha started, then paused and pointed towards the door with her thumb. "I'm on my way out. I just stopped by to grab a plate. That's it. My ride is right around the corner. I was just checking up on my baby real quick. Steve, you gotta forgive her, man. Please forgive her. At least hear her out. Please? Cuz Steve, I'm telling you right now, this girl really do love you," Tasha said, smiling innocently at him before she heard a car horn outside. "Okay, um, I guess I'll see y'all later," she finished before walking swiftly out the door. The door closed. Steve didn't say a word to Angelia. He didn't even really have anything he wanted to say at the moment. He thought of a thousand things to say to her on his ride home, but he didn't feel like saying one damn word right now.

Angelia had cooked one of his favorite meals for him. The aroma filled up every corner of the house, but Steve wasn't having it. Angelia knew what Steve's silence meant, but she knew even more that his refusal to eat his favorite meal meant he was really going through it at the moment, so she didn't push him. She gave him his space.

Steve apathetically went into the other room where he had a blow up mat inside. He dusted it off, and laid down before proceeding to silently cry himself to sleep.

He had only fallen asleep for a few minutes before Angelia came into the room with a plate in her hand.

"You sure you don't want some of this? I know you gone wake up hungry."

"Naw, I'm good," he replied.

"Um . . . okay," she said solemnly and slowly closed the door.

Steve fell back into his sleep again for a much longer period this time. Around 3 o'clock in the morning, Angelia managed to creep back into the room wearing a silky, silhouette-like, cream colored nightgown. It was one of Steve's favorites, and there was never a night where she had worn it that they didn't end up having sex. Angelia walked quietly up to him and sat down beside him. She eased his dick out through his boxers and proceeded to give him head. The sensation had Steve half asleep, half awake. For a second, he genuinely thought he was dreaming, getting the best head of his life, until he woke up to see Angelia's head bopping up and down.

"Stop," he said in a low voice, indicating he was still half asleep. He managed to lift his arms and gently brush Angelia with them, trying to push her away. "I'm straight."

"But, just let me finish," she said, wiping the saliva from her mouth.

"Naw, I'm straight," Steve retorted, becoming even more fully awake. "Why don't you go suck somebody else's dick? You know, like that nigga dick that you was sucking earlier."

"I . . . " Angelia opened her mouth to say something, but her words got caught in her throat. Her eyes did a little dance around before her face sunk into sadness.

"I . . . I didn't suck his dick," she said quietly, as she looked down at the floor humiliated. She then got up and walked out of the room straight to her bed where she collapsed and cried until the tears drained her of all her energy, and she fell asleep. She knew she had messed up really bad, and she wasn't sure what was going to happen with them, but she was hoping, more than anything, that somehow she could fix it.

CHAPTER
EIGHT

Around 9 o'clock that morning, Steve reached his arms over his head and stretched. As he wiped away the sleep from his eyes, he could smell breakfast being cooked. He could hear frying and chopping sounds. The clang of plates hitting together and pans being set down woke him up. While normally the smell of breakfast would have him jumping to his feet, today, he was frankly disgusted by it.

"Oh, so now this bitch suddenly wants to cook breakfast, lunch, and dinner when just 2 weeks ago, I had to beg her just to make me something simple. This shit crazy," he mumbled to himself as he sat up. He got up and went to the bathroom to get himself ready for the day. He showered, gave himself a touch up on his line up, and walked into his room to pick out something to wear. He was going to go see his Uncle Swift in the Feds today. His uncle was serving a 20 year sentence for a murder he was found to be linked to. He had been locked up for about ten years already now. He was basically like a father figure to Steve, and they always talked about everything together. No topics were off the table with Uncle Swift. It had been about 2 years since Steve had last went to visit him, although before that, he had made a point to go visit him at least once a month. While he had been busy at work, there was no excuse that he hadn't made it up there in two years to see the man who was always there for him over the years. He decided that today, he was going to pop in and visit his Uncle. After all, he had been stressing heavy, and needed to get some good advice about what to do with Angelia.

Angelia was in the kitchen when she saw Steve walking toward the door. She dropped everything she was doing and rushed to greet him. Steve threw a glance her way out of the corner of his eye. He almost couldn't believe it. Angelia was, for the first time ever, actually wearing an apron. "Hi, hey, um . . . did you, or are you hungry? I made breakfast. It's um, bacon, eggs, and pancakes if -."

Slam! The door shut behind Steve. She had only turned around for a second to point to the pancakes when she heard the door slam. Her wet hands dropped to her sides in futility, and she soon found herself needing support from the wall to stand, before sliding down its length, and sobbing silently to herself.

Steve drove up to the Federal Prison in Milan City. It was about an hour drive, but the time didn't matter. He was excited to meet with his uncle and see what he had to say. He was actually enjoying the drive, since there was very little traffic, and it gave him a chance to clear his mind and organize some of his thoughts. He wasn't blaring trap music today. He had the windows rolled part of the way down and was breathing in the fresh air of the passing wind. As he pulled off the exit of the freeway to Milan, it occurred to him that he hadn't been paying attention to what he was doing at all, yet somehow it had been a safe, steady, and refreshing drive.

He parked and walked into the visitor's lobby at the prison. He then approached the desk to let them know who he was there to see. When Uncle Swift came out for the visit, he had a smile on his face that stretched from ear to ear. He was absolutely beaming with happiness from seeing his nephew's face. Steve looked at him walking in his direction, and noticed that he looked a little bigger than he remembered. His prison clothes weren't exactly sitting on him the same way anymore. Uncle Swift had increased significantly in body mass, and his clothes would need to be custom tailored in order to fit him properly.

As Swift got close, he stretched his arms out and took the last few steps towards Steve.

"NeeeeeeeeePPPPPPPHHHHHEEEWWWWW! Haha! Come here! What up baby boy? How you doing?" he said as he wrapped his arms around him and hugged him as tightly as he could, then kissed him on his forehead.

Steve smiled. He was just as happy to see Swift as Swift was to see him. He promised himself that he'd never wait this long to visit again.

"What up, Big Unk?" he said as he looked his uncle from head to toe, with more than a little amount of amazement in his face. "Daaaaammmn, you getting big as hell. What you eating in there? Or should I say, what you lifting? You den got huge since the last time I seen you."

Swift laughed. "Nothing too exciting to mention, but yeah, I do be working out daily. It helps keep the mind and body right. In here you gotta stay physically and mentally solid, because a lot of these muthafuckas got bad energy and try to bring you down. I stay above that shit, by working out and doing my own thing," he said, then flexed his arm and held it out. "Muthafucka hard as a rock."

"You telling me. I see that shit," Steve said as he grabbed ahold of Swift's bicep. "Damn, I need to start hitting the gym more. I been slacking. They been working me like a slave out there, but that's no excuse. I gotta make time to do it."

"Yeah, nephew. You'll make time for what's important to you. Remember that. So, you still at the same job?"

"Yeah, I'm hanging in there."

"Well, that's good to hear. I'm very proud of you. You wouldn't believe how many young guys come here to do time and leave, and then you see them come walking through them doors again. Shit's sad."

Steve nodded. Although he hadn't brought anything up yet, Swift could tell that Steve had something on his mind, or that something was bothering him.

"You okay, nephew?" he asked in a quiet, but serious tone.

Steve didn't think that the way he was feeling was so obvious, but Swift could read him like a book. Steve immediately became like a child, and the tears ran down his face uncontrollably. Swift put his arm around him and pulled him in close.

CHAPTER NINE

Swift was 45 years old, and was used to getting bad news, and watching others have their hearts broken. Someone was always dying, overdosing, getting stabbed, murdered, or losing their family and friends while in prison. Although he had no idea what was exactly wrong, he braced himself for the bad news, because he hadn't seen Steve cry since Steve's dad was killed when he was 13 years old. Seeing Steve break down like that made him a little nervous. He knew something had to be seriously wrong.

"What's the matter, nephew? What happened?"

"Man," he began, "I don't even know where to start. Unk, I'm just out here going through it, trying to make it and figure things out. I work every day, bust my ass trying to make some money, but I don't make shit after I pay all my bills and shit. I try to be a good boyfriend, good son to my mom, and my luck is just fucked up. I just don't get it, and I don't know what to do." He sniffed and wiped the tears from his eyes and said, "And I miss my dad." He stopped talking, and continued to cry. Swift waited patiently and held him close to him, while slightly massaging his shoulders to let him know he was there for him, and that he could let it all out. He looked down at Steve, knowing that he had more to say.

Eventually Steve spoke up and said, "I fucking caught my girlfriend in the bed with a nigga at my house. She was in MY bed, getting her back pounded out by some nigga I never seen in my life. I still can't believe that shit. My whole life is in shambles right now."

"Wow," Swift said quietly as his eyes widened a little. He held Steve close as he continued to cry. After taking a moment to think, Swift responded, "Listen, nephew. You gone need to calm down and relax. Life ain't over. Shit, for you, it's just beginning. Nothing is broken that can't be fixed. Look, bad things happen to all kinds of people. Life ain't meant to be easy. It's the storm that makes the sailor, it's the resistance that builds the muscle, you know? The key to this is to deal with it, and come out on the other side stronger than you've ever been before. If you think your life is in shambles, it's gone be in shambles, nephew. It's alright to go through it a little, but you can't think that way. It ain't gone do you no good, that's for sure."

Steve looked at his uncle. "I know, Unk. But damn, I'm hurt over this shit. Hurt bad. I ain't ate since the other day, and I'm still not hungry."

"That's because you love this girl. When things don't go right with the ones you love the most, it's gone hurt. Is this that same girl I met on Facetime with you a few years ago? Is it the same one you said you were going to marry?"

Steve shook his head up and down, sniffed again, and dried his tears.

Swift continued, "She's a beautiful girl, that's for sure. So, I definitely understand how you feel over this. I remember when I was about 28, I was dealing with my first baby momma strong. I was out there getting all this money in the streets, but at the same time, I was fucking all these chicks on the side. I caught a petty ass case where I had to do 6 months in county jail. I left that woman all my money, car, houses, and drugs. I mean, I left her ass everything. Before I got locked up, we was talking about marriage and shit, so the first week they locked me up, I went on and married her in jail. You know what she did? This lady wrote a letter telling me that she's divorcing me and moving away. She didn't even have the decency to talk to me on the phone or visit me about it. At the bottom of the letter she wrote down the names of about 23 different females, I'm talking first and last names, that I had been with while we was together. Don't ask me how she knew, because I still don't know. But, she told me that it was over with us, and she took the kids and disappeared with all my shit! You talking about sick, maaaaannnn, I was throwing up for a whole fucking week." Swift laughed as he thought back about it. "Nephew, women can be vicious, I'm telling you."

Swift's story, and the way he told it, made Steve start laughing. Swift was so wise, but always so animated and funny at the same time. The story eased Steve up a bit and he said, "Did you see her when you got out?"

"Hell no! I couldn't even find her for like 5 years. Shit, my ass was so broke when I came home, I ain't have two quarters to rub together."

They both started cracking up.

"So what you do?" Steve asked as he finally stopped laughing.

"Shit, I did what any man supposed to do. I figured it out. I got my ass a job, hustled, stacked my money up, and made a commitment that I would never ever put myself in a position where a woman could get down on me like that again. She literally took everything, and I was stuck having to figure it out. I was so embarrassed about it, but it made me stronger and wiser. It fucked my head up a lot too, but you know," he finished, laughing.

"What would make a girl want to fuck another dude in the same house she stays at with her boyfriend?"

"I can give you a million reasons why nephew. Are you still with her?"

"I mean . . . yeah. Well, I haven't made my mind up yet about what I should do. I think she only did it because I was working long hours every day, and haven't really been having sex with her much. Then, my money kinda messed up right now too. I almost feel like I've forced her away, so to speak."

"Listen, nephew, when a person shows you who they really are, believe them."

"What you mean by that?"

"Exactly what I said. For example, if someone steals from you, that person is a thief. They showed you who they were by stealing. So if you want to forgive them for stealing, and it happens 1, 2, 3, 4, or 5 years later, you can be mad, but be mad at yourself because that person showed you what they were, a thief. Same is true for a cheater, a slut, a killer, a rat, or whatever. You got it?"

"Damn, so basically you saying my girl will cheat again?"

"Haven't you told me that you caught her on other occasions texting other guys?"

"Yeah . . . over a period of time. One was last year, and there was another one the year before that."

"Right," Swift said, then paused to look at him to make sure he was still listening. "And now, you have caught her having sex in the bed with another man. And there ain't no telling how many times it happened before that you just didn't catch."

CHAPTER TEN

Steve took a big swallow, then looked back at his uncle.

"So, damn, what should I do then?"

"Me? If I were you, I'd definitely leave her ass. Do you cheat on her or deal with other chicks?"

"No. She's like the 4th chick I ever had sex with, ever. I've never cheated on her or gave my number out, or even accepted a number from another female."

"Nephew, you supposed to be fucking out there. Let's trade places and Big Unk can show you how it's done," Swift said, laughing and slapping Steve on the shoulder.

Steve laughed. "I get it, but seriously, Unk. One of my homies said to just get a plug from her because she's Mexican, then leave her ass after I'm all linked up with the plug."

Uncle Swift backed up a little in his seat, looked at Steve with an eyebrow raised, then started laughing.

"Idiot," he finally said, amidst the laughing. "If you get a Mexican plug through her, and it's her family member or someone close to her, there ain't no leaving that woman and still being plugged in." He scratched his head and continued, "Shit, in some cases, there ain't no leaving at all. Alive at least. So you can't listen to them guys out there." Swift shook his head before looking back at Steve. "So, what is it you trying to accomplish with this whole situation?"

"I don't know." Steve looked at the ground, and the smile faded from his face. "I feel like, maybe, if I was making more money, she wouldn't have cheated on me."

Swift laughed again and shook his head. Everything that was coming out of Steve's mouth was killing him. He really didn't get it. "My nephew a certified sucka," he said while laughing. "Come on. For real? I know you ain't say what I think I just heard you say."

Steve looked at him perplexed and replied, "What?"

"You think that more money . . . if you made more money . . . your girl would all of the sudden not cheat anymore? Like you think the whole reason she been cheating is over money?"

"Yeah."

Uncle Swift slapped his own forehead. He was hoping that some of what he had told Steve would have sunken in, but it clearly hadn't. He wanted to help Steve think for himself, and be able to judge people based on their actions, instead of their promises. "Man, do that sound like wifey material to you? Do it? Because what you saying is as long as you down and out, it's okay for her to not be loyal to you and she can cheat, but when you get your money right, all of the sudden she gone magically become loyal and dedicated to the relationship. Do you hear how that shit sounds?"

Steve scratched his neck. Now, things were starting to make sense to him, hearing how his thoughts sounded coming out of someone else's mouth. "Okay, maybe that came out sideways," he said, laughing nervously. "I don't know. I can't explain what I was thinking."

Swift spread out his arms and said, "It's nothing to explain. You clearly love her and want to be with her still even after you saw her getting her back pounded out by another nigga!" He then threw his arms over his head and pretended to faint dramatically in his chair.

Steve was quiet for a few seconds. "Okay, okay. I think I'm ready to move on from her, but I want her to know how I feel. Like I just want to boss up and just shit on her, because she thinks she the shit."

Swift shook his head at the suggestion, then patted him gently on the back.

"Man, that's a childish way of thinking. That ain't you. How about this instead? Move on. You're still young. Get your mind and your money right then get you a better quality woman, not this shit you're currently dealing with. Her ass sounds like a nightmare. What does she do for a living?"

"Nothing right now. She's collecting unemployment."

"That's it? Not taking any classes? She have any skills or is she trying to learn anything?"

"She be doing some modeling stuff here and there, but no schooling or anything like that, no."

Swift slapped his hands on his knees and sat up straight. He had heard enough.

"Nephew, you gotta get you a woman. Angelia is a beautiful girl, but forget all that. Looks fade over time, and then what are you left with? You need someone that's on her shit. You need someone that owns their own shit. Don't let a woman come into your life and live off you like a leech just because she's pretty. There's a million pretty women out there, and being pretty don't pay the fucking bills. You need a woman that's gone have your back while you have hers. A woman that's gone come up there on your lunch break trying to fuck you instead of sitting at home, collecting unemployment, and complaining."

Steve nodded to himself. He couldn't disagree with anything he was hearing. "So, Unk, what do you think I should do about a plug?"

CHAPTER
ELEVEN

Swift paused, then looked around at his surroundings before leaning in a little closer to Steve.

"I think you should help me out with something. If you do that, I will give you a plug in San Antonio, Texas. She's a chick I dealt with for years, and she's about my age. I'll tell you how to find her once you complete what I need you to do."

"Find her? She ain't got a phone number?"

Swift shook his head again. He had a lot to teach him. He was starting to understand why Steve was still stuck at the point he was in his life.

"We don't use phones, nephew. You shouldn't use them either. They're tracking devices, and you don't need to give yourself or your location away that easy."

"What about a throw away? A burner?"

"No such thing. Everything is recorded and can be tracked. I would not chance it either way. No phones."

"Okay, what do you need me to do for you?" Steve asked.

Swift moved in even closer to his nephew. Steve understood that he was about to say something important and confidential, so he sat up as well. Their conversation continued from that point in very low voices.

"I got two kilos of cocaine buried in the backyard of my baby momma house in Alabama, not the one I was just telling you about. All you gotta do is go down there and grab them. It's 98%, so it's very good. Much better than these guys got up here in Pontiac and Detroit. You can make 3 out of each one and it's still going to jump back. Make sure you use really good blenders, small and big ones."

Steve widened his eyes. "Shit."

"Yeah, it's also some cut inside. Only use this cut, nothing else. It's the good shit. I'll tell you what it is later, but it should be about 5 kilos of cut in there as well. If you end up needing more cut, call this number," Swift said as he wrote down a phone number.

"He lives in Detroit and owns a lot of shit. He is about 75 years old, a little short Mexican. Just tell him you're Swift's nephew, and I sent you to get the favor he said he would do for me. He will know what you talking about. Once you sell this, I'ma need you to bring my daughter $100,000, and then deposit $8,000 in my account here."

"You can have all that money in here?"

"Yeah, this the Feds. My homeboy got $90,000 in his. So, you will be giving me about $54,000 per kilo, but you will see that it's well worth it. People are going to go crazy over this shit. Like I said, ain't nobody got anything like it up here. Be careful when you bringing them back from Alabama. Make sure they are hidden and wrapped up tightly. Hiding meaning, stash box type shit, nothing basic. Don't tell anyone where you going or the reason why. Just go and come back. Don't ever ask me about anything over the phone. My baby momma will already know you are coming and for what. After this, make sure you have at least $100,000 cash ready to go to San Antonio. Be safe, be patient, be strategic. Think about what you are doing before you do it. Don't be afraid to use the resources around you. You can't do everything by yourself once this gets going. You are going to need some help, especially once you start working with this Texas play I got for you."

Steve was nervous and excited. He wanted to win, and he was ready. "Should I drive my car to Alabama or get a rental?"

"Don't matter. What kind of car you got now?" Swift asked. "Impala with some 20" rims."

"The new Impala? Them pretty slick."

"Naw, it's a 2005."

"A 2005?" Swift was surprised. "Get rid of the rims too."

"Okay."

"What kind of car your girl got?"

"2005 Ford Fusion I think it is."

"Nephew, you gotta get your swag right. Get you a better whip. If you staying with your girl, she gone need a better one too."

"We own our cars though, Unk."

"They $2,000 a piece. Y'all should own y'all cars. You proud about that?"

"Naw, I'm just saying."

"What you saying?"

"I thought it was better to own your car than to pay a note on it."

"A car holds no value, so I don't care if you own it or not. Get you something better. You will get better chicks, and have a cleaner image if you get something newer. And clean your damn nails too. You all lined up and shit with dirty nails. Where they do that at?"

Steve balled his hands up to hide his nails. "I mean, I don't know."

"Listen man, get YOU together. I'm talking all together, physically, mentally, financially, and even spiritually too. Make your whole self better. Don't just try to look good and get your money up, that'll only get you so far."

"How do I do all that?"

"Read books. Get the 'Rich Dad, Poor Dad' book so you can learn how to invest your money. It'll teach you the difference between an asset and a liability, and you gotta know the difference if you gone succeed. Get you a set scheduled work out time and a membership at a big gym, not a small one. I see you need to get out more, and if you in a gym, you gone at least be around people that's trying to better themselves physically. Start taking care of yourself more. You see what these women out here doing. They getting teeth, ass, titties, and even lips done. They trying to be the best version of themselves. I don't see anything wrong with the ass, teeth, and titties, but the lips . . . that's a lot." He started laughing then continued, "Like damn, girl. You don't like your lips neither?"

They both started cracking up again.

"And I know you not gone like this, but please get some different pussy, nephew. Just do it for me."

Steve laughed.

"I'm trying to figure out how I'ma get the money to go to Alabama. I'm already late on my rent. I got it, I was just trying to flip this last ounce."

"You should be able to spend $500 to get there and back."

"Not with a rental. And then I have to call off work."

"Nephew, quit the job. Sell your car, and get a rental. You got a credit card?"

"Nope."

"You got a bank account?"

"Nope."

"Wow, you really out there living like a bum for real, huh? Listen, when you get to Alabama, tell Lily to give you her daughter's number. She fixes credit, but tell her I said to give you the game so you can do it yourself." Swift took a deep breath, then patted his nephew on the back again. "We got some work to do with you, I see. We going to get you together though, don't worry."

"I can't sell my car, Unk. That's gone be my grinding mobile. I know how to last out there. All them dudes with flashy cars be getting pulled over all the time. I don't want them problems."

"You ain't gotta get a Benz, just a newer, up to date whip."

"Okay."

"One more thing."

"What's that, Unk?"

"If any one of them niggas play with you out there, just mail their full name to that Alabama address, and it's over for them."

"Got it, Unk."

"Let's get this money." He gave Steve a pound. "Oh, and nephew, don't forget to get some new pussy for me."

Steve laughed. "I already got somebody in mind."

CHAPTER
TWELVE

Hours later the correctional officer came by to escort Swift back to his cell. Before Steve's uncle left, he patted Steve on the back gently twice and whispered to him, "You know what to do."

Steve looked up at his uncle and nodded. He was feeling better after all. His uncle had not only given him great advice on what to do about Angelia, but also provided him with a once-in-a-lifetime opportunity to get his money up. He knew talking to his uncle would do him some good, but this was next level. He walked out of the prison feeling like a new man. By the time Steve got back to his car to check his phone, he had 24 missed calls, 16 voicemails, and 22 text messages, and all of them were from Angelia. She had texted him a book telling him sorry a thousand different ways. Steve started checking the messages one by one. In every single one of her voicemails, she was begging him for forgiveness.

Most of them sounded identical. His phone started ringing while he was checking and reading through her messsages. Steve made a face when he saw her name and number pop up on his phone. The first thing he was going to do once he got off the phone was delete the heart emoji next to her name. "What's up? Damn, you filled my voicemail up like it was an emergency."

"Why you wasn't answering?"

"I was busy visiting my uncle in the Feds."

"Oh, sorry. I thought you was ignoring me on purpose. Did you read my texts?"

"I haven't had a chance. I just got back to my phone, and you called."

"Okay," she said then went silent.

"I'll call you back," he said, then hung up.

He started his car, and turned up the radio. Within minutes, he was merging onto the freeway. While he drove, he thought a lot about what his uncle had said. He was excited, and was bobbing his head to the music, really feeling himself despite the terrible day he had yesterday. After driving for about 25 minutes, he was close to Detroit, and he turned his head around as he saw a Monte Carlo that looked just like the one that was in his driveway yesterday pass by in the other direction. He couldn't help but be struck by it. It had to be the same car. He tried to ignore it, just driving forward, and then he looked in his rear view mirror. He couldn't ignore it after all. He made a u-turn instantly, squealing his tires, and started to follow the car.

He followed him for about 15 minutes. At first, he was real committed to tailing the car, but then he started to get tired after he noticed the vehicle's driving pattern. It had no real direction. The driver and the passenger were just going around in circles, showing off. Steve still stuck with the car, even though it was speeding on the side streets, and leaving smoke at each stop sign.

Finally, he followed the car to a side street back onto a main road, and it came to a stop at a restaurant. The Monte Carlo parked in the parking lot, and Steve stopped a safe distance away where he could still see. He knew there was a possibility that this dude might have a gun on him, but he was going to see how close he could get to him. The driver and the passenger sat in the car for a few minutes, and Steve couldn't see what they were doing in the car. He kept watching, and eventually, he got out of the car wearing a black tank top, with at least three cuban link chains hanging around his neck. Between the neckpieces and the watch, Steve couldn't tell which was glistening more. The guy had on a designer belt, but was still sagging, showing off his designer boxers as well. Steve saw him run inside the restaurant, and the woman in the passenger seat stayed back in the car. He started his engine again, pulled around back, and walked around the front to where the dude's car was parked. He peeked inside the window of the restaurant and saw him paying for his food. Steve could feel his heartrate start to rise. He had a little something he wanted to give this dude, and the more he watched him, the more his desire to get at him increased. He saw the guy nod his head, and walk out the door with his bag of food. As he made his way toward his car, Steve was determined about what he was going to do. Steve walked towards the man at a slow pace, and just before he passed him, he swiftly and suddenly punched him in the face, knocking him flat on his back. Steve then looked down at him. He was out cold. He wanted to snatch his chains and his watch off of him, but there were people in their cars, and coming in and out of the restaurant, so he jogged around the back and got in his car. He pulled out on the main road, and immediately called James. "What's up, bro?"

Steve let out two big breaths. He was excited and breathing heavily. "Aye . . . why I'm in Detroit and just seen that nigga I caught fucking Angelia yesterday." He let out a few more big breaths.

"Oh, yeah?"

"Yeah, and this time I knocked that nigga out!"

James laughed. "For what, bro? You starting more unnecessary shit out there."

"Naw, he didn't even recognize me. Nigga was not even looking for real when I hit him in his shit."

"You crazy bro."

"That nigga got down on me. I had to get him back. I had slipped on the damn sheet that was on the hardwood floor when I swung on him at the crib."

"You happy now?" James asked, laughing his ass off.

"Hell yeah." Steve laughed also. He started to feel even better as he thought about the dude laying there out cold on the concrete.

"What you up to?"

"Just left the federal prison. I was up there visiting Unk."

"How is he?"

"He good. That nigga big as hell now. He buff as fuck."

James laughed. "Okay, Unk. He gone get out and be fucking all the young hoes. I know the nigga looking youthful in the face too."

"Hell yeah. He looking healthy as hell in there, like he really onto something. Shit he doing better in prison than I am out here in the world. How the fuck?"

They both laughed and hung up the phone a few minutes later. Steve was definitely in a much better mood than he was when he woke up that morning. He couldn't help but smile as he turned the radio all the way up, and sped down the street.

CHAPTER
THIRTEEN

Angelia had been sitting at home all morning, thinking about what she had done and how she could fix it. She had been waiting on her friend Esha's plane to land, so she could tell her the news, but it seemed like it was taking forever. The morning was dragging on and on. She stared at the TV mindlessly, until her phone finally rang.

"Damn, I'm glad I wasn't dying. I told you it was an emergency," Angelia said.

Esha giggled. "You is silly. Naw, my phone went dead. I asked you did anybody die and you said no, it was about you and Steve. What happened? I'm sorry."

"I got caught having sex with Jon Jon."

Esha stopped walking. "What! Where? How?"

"Girl, at the house, my house."

"I told you to stop letting him come over there! Your ass do not know how to cheat. I knew he was gone find out eventually. You lucky you got away with it this long. So, what he say? What happened? How did he catch you? Tell me the tea."

Angelia giggled. "He tried to fight Jon Jon and failed, but now it's super awkward with us and I don't know what to do."

"Jon Jon beat him up?" Esha asked.

"Yeah, no, kinda yeah."

Esha spit out all the juice in her mouth as she burst out in laughter. At that moment, a white woman happened to be walking by the line of Esha's explosion. She received the bulk of Esha's drink on her bag, with some of it on her clothes. She looked at Esha, clearly agitated. Esha tried to look as remorseful as possible, and began to dig in her bag to try and find something to help out with. "Oh, my God. I am sorry, lady." She started to dab the lady's bag with her napkin, but the lady didn't say a word. She just stood there mad. After Esha cleaned off what she could from the bag and her clothes, the woman walked away, fuming with anger at a very fast pace. Esha stood there watching her as she walked away. "Girl, this white lady about to kick my ass! You made me spit my juice all over her."

"She will be okay."

"This all because your ass went and got caught getting your cheeks clapped. You done fucked it up with Steve now. He is going to beat your ass this time. You messed up bad."

Angelia sounded worried as she said, "You think so?"

"Yes! He caught y'all fucking like fucking in the act?"

"Doggy style, I was yelling and everything, girl."

Esha erupted with laughter again. "Plus he got his ass beat. Bitch, pack your bags now! Did he leave yet?"

"No, that's what I'm saying. He hasn't left yet, and neither did I. We been texting though. It feels like he might stay around, I don't know. I'm so sick though, girl. I've been cooking like crazy, hoping he'll eat, and I have been throwing it all away. I really don't know what to do."

"Just relax and let him come to you. Don't try to force him to talk about it right now too much. He's probably pissed off and really want to beat your ass. Angelia, you did the ultimate! Damn, I can't believe he caught you like that."

"I know. Neither can I. It's horrible even thinking about it." Angelia started getting sad again.

"Me and you both know he's pissed. What man wouldn't be, especially one that loves your dirty drawls? I would leave if I were you. He's not going to let that slide. He probably scorned from that happening. Oh, Lord! You done turned another good man bad out here, Angelia!"

"Whatever! You told me to try something different when I told you how I felt about Steve and him being content with working that weak ass job."

Esha shook her head. "Woah, whoa, fucking whoa! I didn't tell your ass to get caught. You said you wanted someone that would motivate you to want more, do more, and see the world and all this other shit. I told you that I feel you, then I was mentioning all the guys I be dealing with and what they be on, and your ass went crazy."

Angelia giggled. "No, no, no. I just think I am more attracted to guys who run things and take charge. Like with Steve, everything I say he basically listens to and does. But I want a guy that already knows what to do and does it. Like Steve will ask me if he can eat my pussy. I don't like that. Jon Jon, on the other hand . . . we can be walking up the stairs and he will just pull my pants down, push me down, and start eating that shit from the back."

Both of them laughed.

"I feel you on that. Well, Steve is definitely not that. You told me before, you always have to initiate when y'all have sex, and I already knew what you was dealing with. But I like that. I don't want a man touching me unless I'm giving him some type of signal to. Jon Jon would piss me off, walking up the stairs and he want to all of a sudden eat some pussy," Esha said and started giggling. "The good thing is, you can have the best of both worlds. You just have to find it or train Steve how to be it. That choice is up to you."

"I tried, and he don't listen to me. He thinks he knows everything. I don't know. I think I want to leave, but I'm just scared to. I've had a boyfriend for so long, I think it would be weird."

Esha couldn't relate to what she was saying. "Can't say that's me. I like to be single, that way I can do what I want, when I want, and how I want."

Angelia giggled. "I don't even know why I am talking to you. We like day and night. Your ass don't even care about none of the dudes you deal with."

"Sure don't. They all dogs. I don't trust none of them," Esha said.

They giggled.

"But Steve not like them, he a good dude. But if you not feeling it, you gone have to move on. But don't be mad when you see him in another relationship with someone else, making babies and shit."

Angelia giggled. "I think me and Jon Jon can work."

"Work what?"

"In a relationship."

"Girl, please! That nigga got nothing but hoes."

"He's handsome. He got money, no kids, loves his parents, and I love the way he treats me and makes me feel. I think he will stop messing with all his girls for me. Just the conversation we be having and what he be on is just way different from Steve."

"I mean, y'all have been dealing with each other for a while now. You just make sure that's what you really want to do. It does seem like you've gotten bored with Steve these last couple years. So, if you not happy with him, just leave him. Don't scorn that man."

Esha finished on that note. She had already been to school with so many guys who were all really sweet at the time; boys that were precious and were complete lover boys in school, but now had become total savages, heartbreakers, and heartless people because one girl broke their heart when they had given her nothing but love. She hated to think that Steve could become one of those guys too. As much as she'd like to support Angelia and her decisions, she still felt like Angelia didn't always make the best choices. Steve was a good guy, the kind of man a girl would want to settle down with. Steve was supposed to be that man for Angelia, but here she was, talking about being in a working relationship with Jon Jon. Esha was willing to bet her bottom dollar that Jon Jon was fucking someone else right now, as they spoke, but Angelia would have to learn that for herself. After all, she already tried to tell her that Jon Jon was a player, but Angelia was the type that needed to learn things the hard way.

CHAPTER
FOURTEEN

Steve set his alarm for 4 o'clock the following morning, and he got right out of bed when it went off. He sat on the edge of the bed for a moment to gather his thoughts, then went into the bathroom to clean himself up. He jumped in the shower and washed himself off while he thought about the long day he had ahead of him. Making it to Alabama was going to take him most of the day, so he wanted to get out the door nice and early. As he finished up brushing his teeth, Angelia woke up and noticed him in front of the bathroom mirror.

"You leaving for work already? You want breakfast?"

"Naw, going out of town. I'll be back in a couple days."

"Out of town?" Angelia sounded concerned. She sat up and turned to face Steve. "Why haven't you been going to work?"

Steve didn't even look in her direction when he replied, "I quit. I got better plans now." He took a swig of mouthwash, and swished it around in his mouth while Angelia kept talking.

"Better plans? What better plans? Come on, you know we need to pay the rent. Another letter came in yesterday, and it went up

$150 more with the late charges. We gotta do something about that. The rent payments ain't just gone go away."

He had little desire to listen to what she had to say about anything. "Yeah, I know," he replied while walking out of the bathroom. "I'll pay it when I get back." He didn't even look at her when he continued, "If you'll excuse me now." He walked by her grabbing a duffle bag of clothes that was sitting on the edge of the bed and walked out the bedroom door.

"Safe travels," Angelia said as the door closed behind him. She started to wonder what Steve was actually doing. He had never been one to be ambiguous with her when it came to the details of what he had going on. It was obvious that she was reaping some of the consequences of her actions, and yet, as much as she couldn't bring herself to admit it, she was trying to make moves to save this relationship. A few minutes later, she picked up her phone and sent Steve a text saying that she will have some money coming in next week if he needed help with the rent. When Steve opened the text, a big smirk stretched across his face. He couldn't bring himself to reply appropriately to Angelia's message, so all he did was like it, then put his phone down.

Steve got in his car and called Shila to let her know he was on his way. She had messaged him on Facebook right after the incident they had at the gas station and told him she wanted to give him some pussy still. She left her number for him in the message, and he had texted her. All through the day before, she had been sending him naked pics of herself and telling him what she wanted to do to him. Although he knew that she had some kind of weird vendetta against Angelia, he still wanted something new, and this was the only thing on the menu at the moment. Plus, he wanted to try to listen to Swift's advice.

Although James had heard a lot of stories about Shila being with different men, that didn't change the fact that she favored Kevin

Hart's wife, the light skinned one, very attractive, and just a couple inches shorter. Steve drove to her place wondering if she was going to do some of the freaky shit she was saying to him. Either way, it was going to be on once he got there, and it had been years since he had been with any woman other than Angelia. He had his window down and the cold morning air rushed into the car. Part of him was a little nervous, since he felt out of practice. When he pulled into her neighborhood, all the houses looked either brand new, or like they had been built in the last few years. As he drove, he looked at the houses, and they all looked very nice. Most of them were two story homes with nice landscaping done in the front yards. Some of them had swimming pools with large decks off the back of the homes. Others had beautiful brick patios that led to fire pits in the back yard. He continued following his GPS to the front of her house. It was still dark outside, but it helped that she had left the garage door open for him and told him to park inside. Steve drove in and parked next to her Mercedes SUV. He hadn't even gotten out of his car yet when he saw Shila, standing by the door in a white silk gown with a pony tail pulled to the back. Even in the low light, he could tell that her gown was significantly transparent. He checked her out a little bit longer. She looked very attractive, to say the least. She had a natural beauty where it didn't take much for her to look good.

Once he stepped out, she put the garage door down. He walked inside and followed her up to her room. He noticed kid toys scattered in the living room. Although it was dark, it was nice and clean smelling inside. He started to feel slightly nervous again, as he thought about how he hadn't been with another chick besides Angelia. He already felt guilty about cheating, but he was just going to go with it.

"Oh, I meant to ask you if you wanted some coffee, or something to wake you up? I know it's early," she said to him with a smile.

"You got a shot of liquor or something?"

"I do. Hold on a second, I'll go grab it."

"Damn, she got some taste," he said quietly to himself after she walked out of the room and he looked around. She had a huge king size bed, and everything matched from the dressers, nightstands, bedding, and even the artwork on the wall. It all went together perfectly. On the wall, a 70" TV was mounted. Slow Jams were playing on the dark screen at a low volume. Soon, she came back with a double shot glass.

CHAPTER
FIFTEEN

T his Patron. It's a little more than a shot," she said, smiling.

"Perfect." He threw it back and shook his head and made an ugly face. The straight tequila entering his body this early in the morning shocked his senses. "You have a nice place," he told her.

"Thank you," she said, and then her eyes did a little dance as she checked him out from head to toe. Steve thought it was sexy. Shila then walked up to him and took the glass out of his hand. She set it on the table, then took Steve's hands and pulled him towards her. Shila looked at him for a moment, and then proceeded to kiss him softly. Her lips melted completely into his.

"Come here," she whispered as she pulled him over to the bed and sat him down at the edge. She began taking his shirt off over his head. She gently kissed his chest once, then pulled down his sweats and boxers to his ankles. He could tell that she loved eye contact. She then grabbed one of the square pillows from the bed and put it on the floor for knee support. She dropped down slowly, while still looking him in the eyes and rubbing his thighs, and then she kissed the tip of his dick softly. He was already fully erect when she licked the head of it, and then she attempted to put as much of his dick as she could in her mouth, just to see if it will fit.

Steve let out a quiet moan as she got close to the bottom of his dick with her lips. She couldn't take the whole length in, so she then began sucking on it gently, taking her time. She ran her tongue from the bottom to the top repeatedly. She licked every part of his shaft, then even kissed and licked his thighs, while stroking his dick at a slow speed. He was already lost from the moment she was playing with the tip, and now he had to support himself by resting his hands on the bed. He watched her as she worked on him, and let out quiet, long sighs of pleasure every now and then.

"Damn, you doing that," he whispered, confirming how good it felt to him.

She smiled at him and whispered back, "You like the way that feel?"

"Yeah," he replied, a little out of breath. Shila repeated her little pattern one more time, and then Steve sat up just so he could run his hands through her hair and around her head. He enjoyed watching her as she bobbed up and down on his shaft.

She slowly stood up, and then pushed him slightly on his chest with her finger. "Scoot back to that pillow up there," she instructed. Steve scooted back on the bed as she pulled his sweats the rest of the way off his legs. She kept her gown on, but raised it up just above her thigh gap. She then crawled between his legs and inserted his dick back in her mouth, and began sucking it gently again until it was rock hard. Steve could tell she loved giving head, the way she was taking her time. He wasn't sure if it was the liquor or her that made him feel so relaxed and comfortable. He just loved the way he felt at the moment.

Shila continued licking and kissing all over his dick. Then she went a little further down and started sucking on his balls, licking and sucking softly, making his balls incredibly wet. She kept it going while massaging his dick up and down, making sure it stayed hard. She licked the creases between his legs and balls, and that drove him crazy, making his dick harder than a brick. She had him going, and she started to produce moans while she was deep throating his dick in and out of her warm mouth.

Steve was in complete ecstasy. He couldn't feel any teeth. It was all wet, warm, and soft inside her mouth, and he was in the clouds trying as hard as he could not to cum. He was curious as to what she tasted like, so he used his hands to hint what he was wanting to do to her.

"Let me rub that ass," he whispered to her, and she smiled, turned, and got on the side of him, not taking his dick out of her mouth. He slowly pulled up her silky gown and ran his hand on the surface of her ass, then gave it a little smack. Her butt was soft like a pillow. Steve massaged it a little bit more, then ran his hands between her legs and felt a puddle. Since he didn't usually mess around with chicks outside of Angelia, he had to do a little smell test, discretely running his hand by his nose, just to check if it was safe. He smelled nothing.

He double checked the puddle again, just to be sure, and it was water. He continued rubbing between her lips for a few more seconds before he motioned her to sit on his face while she was still making love to his dick with her mouth. Shila obliged. Each one of her soft thighs went on both sides of his face. He was now faced with the entirety of it. He began kissing on her thigh first, making his way closer to her pussy. She smelled so fresh and clean, which he loved, so he licked around and in between her pussy lips slowly, making his way up to her clit. When his tongue touched the inside of her lips, she jumped a little, so of course, he went back inside and continued licking nonstop until streams of juices started creeping out and splashing against his tongue and mouth. His tongue dancing around her insides drove her crazy to the point she could not even suck his dick anymore. She was too distracted. All she could do was ask for more of what he was doing. "Oh, my God, baby, yes!" she moaned out over the music playing in the background. "Yes, baby, yes!" she moaned as she felt his tongue dive inside her pussy again, as he ate and sucked the juices out of her. Steve knew exactly what he was doing, and exactly how to do it. "My God, baby yes. Don't stop!" she yelled as he continued sucking. He then went back to her clit, and started licking faster and faster, until he started to feel her body tightening up. "I'm fucking cumming! Ouuu, don't stop! Baby yes . . . yes . . . yeessss!" She was now climaxing as she screamed and rolled her eyes to the back of her head. She exploded then collapsed on top of him. "Oh, my god! You know how-."

Before she was done complimenting Steve, her speech was cut off when she felt his tongue stabbing lightly inside her pussy once again. "Wow," she sighed, while shaking. She moaned, still breathing heavily. She had to grip the sheets and dig her teeth into the bed, because Steve's work on her body was feeling a little too good. Her face then turned sideways on the bed as she tried to restrict herself from screaming too loud, waking her kids up. Tears of joy filled her eyes, until she got to the point where she couldn't take the pleasure anymore. She let out a sharp gasp and then crawled away, her body glistening with sweat in the dimly lit room. "Wait, wait, wait. You gotta stop, and hold on for a second," she said, breathing and laughing at herself from having to run away from the pleasure.

Steve laughed too. He got up and grabbed her from behind, spreading her ass cheeks, bending her over and licking all between her ass crack. "Ouu, shit," she said as she looked back at him. She then arched up more for him. His gentle licks on her ass felt like pure heaven to her, like the calm after the storm. He had her so wet, and that double shot of Patron had him feeling good.

Steve got up and put two of his fingers in Shila's mouth and turned her over. She licked them until they were wet and sloppy, then he pulled them off her tongue and rubbed them against her pussy lips. He then got up and put his dick against her pussy lips, stroking and teasing her slowly. After a few seconds, he thrusted the length of him into her from behind and started stroking in and out of her, slowly at first, but steadily increasing in speed.

"Yes, hit this pussy, baby," she moaned, pushing her ass on his thighs. Other than the sound of the music, all that could be heard was the repetitive 'smack, smack, smack' sound of her ass slapping against him. Each time her ass hit him, it jiggled, and he yanked her thighs back toward his dick over and over again. "Don't stop, baby. Yes! I'm fucking cumming again!" she shouted a little louder than she should have, and he kept pounding her pussy as hard as he could while the sweat dripped from his face and chest down in between them. He didn't stop until he felt himself right on the edge of exploding.

He pulled out of her as he said, "Turn around! Turn around and get this nut!" He was short of breath and holding his dick when she spun around and put her mouth over the end of his dick. "Ahhhh shit! Shit! Get it all, baby, shit!" he growled, releasing all of his sperm inside her mouth. He felt his body go weak with the release. It was as if the stress and weight of the last few days left his body.

CHAPTER
SIXTEEN

"Sheesh!" he said, falling back onto her soft bed. "I needed that." He was breathing heavy and sweating.

"Me too. You got me over here still shaking. I was not expecting all that."

He laughed. "All what?"

"You being able to eat some pussy, and having a nice sized dick and knowing what to do with it. I see why Angelia been with your ass for years now," she joked and giggled. "It all makes sense now," she said before plopping on the bed next to him and laying on her back.

Steve turned to look at her. "Whatever, we about to break up."

"About fucking time," Shila added, unapologetically. "You need somebody real like me anyway. She a lazy bum bitch that's just cute. Kinda cute, because to me she actually funny looking, but whatever."

Steve almost wanted to laugh. "Chill out, chill out. Why you be going so hard on her like that? You don't like her?"

"Nope, hate her."

"For what?"

Shila shrugged. "She's just a sneaky bitch. I don't like her."

Steve could tell that she didn't want to elaborate. He stared at her for a moment, then laid down, thinking to himself, still trying to catch his breath. "How many kids you got? I seen toys and some kid shit downstairs."

"I got two, 4 and 7."

"Same daddies?"

"No, I wish, because my last baby daddy ain't shit."

Steve laughed. "I thought you had about 4 kids."

"Hell no! What you want to give me twins or something?"

He laughed. "Naw, I ain't ready for no kids. Fuck all that."

Shila took his hand and then squeezed it. "So where your dude at?"

"Laying in the bed with me," she replied, raising an eyebrow.

He laughed. "I know you ain't talking about the nigga with the old Impala," he said sarcastically.

She giggled. "That's easy to change. I was talking shit because you were trying to play me like a bum bitch."

"No, I wasn't. I just said I had a girlfriend, that's all."

Shila rolled her eyes. "I should take you from her. She don't even deserve you anyway. That bitch ain't shit."

"Damn, that's how you really feel?"

"Gone and come over here. Let me upgrade you," she told him while putting her hand on his chest. "Be that faithful to a bitch like me and watch what I do for you. I don't even be understanding how sneaky bitches like her be having dudes like you wrapped around their fingers. Drives me crazy, I swear."

Steve wanted to confront the issue head on with her right now. She clearly had a real hatred toward Angelia. "What she done did to you? Talk to me."

"Damn, you nosey, Steve!" she said, smiling and pushing him away playfully. "I just don't like the bitch. Can we just leave it at that?"

Steve watched her for a moment. He didn't feel that was the full truth about why she hated her, but he didn't want to push the issue. "Yeah, we can leave it like that," he said and then paused for a moment. "And . . . we can keep this on the hush. Me and her still together. I don't need any more headaches right now."

"No worries. You gonna be mine eventually anyway," she said with a big grin on her face.

He laughed. "Oh? You think so, huh?"

"I only speak what I know, boo. You didn't know I had a crush on you in high school?"

"Ummm, no. I didn't. I had no idea."

"Yeah, I did, like big time. I used to come to all your football games and everything, but you were with that white girl . . . I forgot her name."

"Tiffany?" he replied.

"Yup, that's the one. So I didn't think you liked chicks that wasn't white, that's why I never said anything to you. All the girls used to want your ass. Man, they was all waiting in line to try and get a piece of you, but you weren't having any of that shit. You was always loyal to your girl, and all them girls knew it too."

He laughed as he noticed the sun coming up over the horizon and lighting up the room. The sunlight snapped him back to reality. He had something important to do, and he couldn't be playing around all day. "Let me get up. I gotta hit this road," he said, leaning over her and giving her a kiss on the lips. "I'll be back in a few days, so I'll holla at you." He put on his clothes, and headed out the door.

Shila followed him when he got up and watched him until he backed out of the driveway. She was already infatuated with him. Steve could tell. He thought it was nice, but maybe a little bit creepy too, especially since she knew he still had a girlfriend. It had him wondering. As he thought about what it would be like to get with Shila, he realized that a lot of additional things came with getting together with her, like her kids and all that. Still, he couldn't help but wonder if maybe that was what he needed, at least at the moment. His thoughts of her continued to linger as he got on the freeway to head out of town. He shook his head to try and shake away these ideas. Now wasn't the time to worry too much about women.

CHAPTER
SEVENTEEN

Steve drove nonstop all the way to Birmingham, Alabama. The ride there was relaxing, but long. He listened to music, and stopped a couple times to get gas and stretch his legs. No matter what he did, he could not stop himself from thinking about what had happened in the early hours of the morning with Shila. He couldn't believe that he had actually had sex with a girl other than Angelia. Although he caught her cheating, he still felt bad for what he did. But Shila was, evidently, actually way cooler than he originally thought, and she had her shit together. It started to make him look at Angelia a little differently, because they were both the same age, and they weren't even close to being on the same level. Shila had two kids, and was still doing great. Angelia didn't have any real responsibilities and she wasn't doing anything. He wanted to keep doing his homework on Shila to see what she was really about, but so far, she didn't seem to be anything like what James was making her out to be.

As he got closer to Swift's baby mother's house, he called her and told her he was about to pull up. When Steve arrived at the house, Lily was in the driveway getting ready to leave in her truck. Steve threw a glance in her direction when he pulled up. She was wearing a long, flowery gown with little polka dots all over it and flat slippers. She looked very casual and comfortable.

"You got somewhere to be?" Steve asked, parking and getting out of the car in a hurry.

"Yeah, I have to meet contractors for this house I am working on, but how you doing? You grew up to be a handsome man," she said as she smiled and gave him a big hug.

"Thank you," he replied.

"You welcome. You got a nice bit of work ahead of you, but there's a shovel over there. Let me show you where you need to dig."

He followed her with the shovel to her back yard behind a nice, large shed that matched the house. "This area right here is where you need to be," she said, pointing to a spot on the ground. "It's about 4 feet deep, but you will see it. It's like a heavy duty black bag. Make sure you fill the hole back in once you finish."

"Okay, I got you. No problem. Thank you. Oh, and Swift said something about your daughter do credit, fixes it or something?"

"Oh yeah, CeCe will get you together. Let me give you her number. I'll call her and tell her you're going to give her a call," she added, pulling out her phone.

"You can tell her to pull up if she's able to. Seems like I'ma be digging here for a minute."

She started looking through her phone to pull up her daughter's contact.

"Okay, I will ask her. Let me see," she said, then started calling CeCe. Right away, CeCe picked up. "Where you at baby?"

"At home working, why? What's up?"

"Swift's nephew from Michigan wanted to meet you, so he can talk to you about credit before he leaves today if you got time."

"Tell her Swift said give me the game," Steve added.

Lily giggled. "He talking about Swift told him to tell you to give him the game."

CeCe giggled, remembering how Swift had always been with her. He had even bought her her first car. He was like a father figure to her.

"Okay, where y'all at?"

"At home. I have to leave though, but he'll be over here waiting for you."

"Okay, I'll be over there in like 30 minutes."

"Okay, baby. Talk to you later," she said before hanging up. "She said 30 minutes. You will still be digging."

He laughed. "Okay, cool. Thanks."

"You welcome, sweetie. It was nice seeing you. Just in case you not here when I come back have a safe trip back. Call me if you need anything."

"Okay, I will. Nice seeing you too," he said before he stuck the shovel in the ground. Steve was starting to understand why Swift was particularly fond of Lily, and her daughter. They both came across like really pleasant people, and he hadn't even met CeCe yet.

Lily had a privacy fence around her whole back yard. Steve watched her leave, and then started digging. Every few minutes, he would look around for a minute, then go back to digging. About 25 minutes later, he was dripping sweat, and still at it when he saw a truck pull up in the driveway. It was the same truck Lily had been driving, but just a different color. CeCe stepped out. She was dark skin, about 5'6" with thick hips and a lot of ass. She complimented her nice figure with fitted black jeans, and a white fitted shirt. She wore a simple pair of sneakers. Steve took a break from digging and watched her as she walked up.

CHAPTER
EIGHTEEN

"Hey, I'm CeCe," she said, extending her hand with a smile.

At first, Steve smiled and reached out his hand, but realized it was covered with dirt. He pulled his hand back quickly. "My hands are filthy, but I'm Steve. How you doing? What kinda truck is that? Is that the same one your mom was driving too?"

"Yeah," she replied, looking back at her truck. "That's the new Ram 1500, and yes, my mom has the same one. She wanted the black, but I really liked the grey for myself." She giggled then looked back at Steve.

"Them nice. What they giving them away or something?" he joked.

"Basically," she said with a smile. "I can get you one if you want. It's only $10,000 for 2 years, then you gotta give it back."

Steve nodded approvingly. "That don't sound too bad. It will be in my name?" he asked as he stuck his shovel back into the dirt and threw out a few more scoops.

"Of course it will be in your name. How's your credit looking?"

Steve looked up at her and wiped the sweat off his face. "No idea. Terrible, I'm assuming. I honestly don't know."

She giggled. "Have you ever had anything in your name that you stopped paying for?"

He threw another scoop of dirt out, and thought for a minute. "Naw, just utility bills. Nothing that I know of . . . wait, yes I do. I have a car on there, and some furniture shit on there."

"That don't mean it's terrible. I can still get you the truck. You want one today?"

Steve's eyes lit up as he thought about having a brand new truck. "I'd love to, but naw, I ain't ready yet. I need like a couple weeks."

"Okay, that's cool. My momma said you live in Michigan, right?"

"Yeah."

"I can have it delivered to you up there. What color you gonna want?"

"White."

"Okay, I got you. Put my number in your phone. I'ma get you the top of the line edition too. It's gone be fully loaded. I love these trucks."

"Bet," he said, handing her his phone.

"So you want me to fix your credit for you too or you just wanna know how to do it?"

"Hmm, tell me how first. Let me see how hard it is."

They both laughed.

"It's not hard. There are just some tedious things you have to do, that's all. Once you know what to do though, it's real easy."

"I feel like I may need to take some notes."

"Yes, you will, for sure. You got my number now. I know you busy at the moment, so we can set up a call for next week or something. That'll give you time to find a time where you can write everything down."

"Yeah, that would be better for sure. Thank you."

"You welcome. No problem at all. Well, Steve, it was nice meeting you. I'll let you finish what you're doing, but make sure you call me any time if you have questions or need any kind of help."

"Okay, I will," he said. As she turned around, the huge rock on her finger caught his eye. Steve smiled, then went back to digging. She waved goodbye as she got back in her truck.

After she left, Steve continued to dig and dig. It was taking longer than he expected. He was sweating, and his back and hands were getting sore. He was definitely getting a good back workout. Lily had said 4 feet, but he felt like he was further down than that already. Eventually, he saw what appeared to be a piece of a black strap sticking up through the dirt. A big smile came across his face, and he felt a second wind come over him. He started digging faster, and tossing the dirt to the other side of the hole. Soon, he was able to pull the bag out.

He opened the bag to take a look inside. "Sheeesh!" he said when he saw what looked like exactly what his uncle told him would be in there. There were 2 kilos wrapped up, and a separate wrapped pack that contained the cut, but it looked like cocaine as well. He wasn't going to question it though. His plan was to follow his uncle's instructions.

Steve took the bag and stashed it in his car, then went back and filled in the hole by the shed. He was glad that it was much faster and took significantly less effort to fill it back in.

The next morning after spending time stashing everything, he got right in his car, and headed straight back to Michigan. The ride home seemed like it was taking a lot longer than the drive down there. He made sure to set his cruise control, and focused on everything he was doing. Although he was nervous, he kept telling himself that he made it down there fine, and he was going to make it back the same way. The ride back was pretty much open freeway, and everything was starting to look the same. Hours later he felt himself getting tired, and shook his head to try to keep himself awake. It didn't work. He turned up his music a little more, and that didn't help either, so he decided it was time for a break. He got off the freeway, and pulled into a gas station that had a fast food restaurant attached to it. When he got out of the car, he stretched his arms over his head. His legs felt like jelly from sitting for so long. He first went into the restaurant and grabbed himself a chicken sandwich, then walked into the gas station. He wasn't normally one to drink much caffeine, but he couldn't afford falling asleep on the road, so he grabbed a few energy drinks, and went back to his car. He stood there eating his sandwich outside his car, taking swigs of his energy drink between each couple bites. After he felt like he had a long enough break, he got back in the car, and let out a long sigh. He wasn't looking forward to the remainder of the drive. A handful of hours later, it was about 2 o'clock in the morning. Steve thought about how he hated driving this late at night with what he had on him, but he only had about an hour to go. He cracked his other energy drink and slammed it. Before he knew it, he was pulling up in his driveway.

CHAPTER
NINETEEN

It was about 3 o'clock in the morning when he pulled up, and he grabbed his bag, walked straight to the guest room, and passed out. When he woke up around noon, his phone was vibrating. It was Shila texting him. He ignored it and got up to brush his teeth.

"Good morning," Angelia said, walking up behind him.

"Good morning," he mumbled, through a mouth full of toothpaste.

"How was your trip?"

"It was good. Everything went good."

"So what are we going to do, keep ignoring each other?"

He spit the toothpaste out of his mouth, and proceeded to rinse off his toothbrush while saying, "I ain't ignoring you. I just ain't got much to say to you. I'm really still in shock over what happened. Do you know how it feels to find someone you love having sex behind your back with someone else . . . in your house?"

She put her head down. "No," she responded quietly.

"It hurts, really bad. It's fucked up, like real fucked up," he said as he put his tube of toothpaste back in the drawer. He still wasn't making eye contact with Angelia. He could see her in the mirror behind him, but hadn't turned around to look at her.

"I'm sorry, Steve. I really am, and I understand that you mad at me, but I want to be with you and only you. And I want you to know that I would never ever let that happen again, ever."

"One time is bad enough, but how can I be sure that it won't happen again? You probably been fucking other niggas for years behind my back. Why didn't you just break up with me instead of doing me like that? I don't understand you. Are you trying to hurt me on purpose or are you just not happy with me?"

There was a prolonged silence from Angelia. She stood there, and he finally turned around to look at her. "Answer me, Angelia. Tell me the truth," he said, then turned back around to wash his face while she thought about a response.

Steve had finished washing his face, and began rinsing it before she replied, "I'm not trying to hurt you at all."

"So why was you fucking another man in this house?" He dried his face off, then turned around to look at her while leaning back on the counter.

"Nothing that I'ma be able to say to you will make sense because you are not a woman. I was feeling unwanted and unneeded, and I feel like you was looking elsewhere, so I looked elsewhere too."

Steve shook his head. He couldn't believe what he was hearing. "The thing is, I wasn't looking elsewhere. And I definitely wasn't bringing another woman into our house, into our bed." He paused for a minute then said, "How long has it been going on, Angelia?"

"What?"

"Your little fling with this dude."

"We have been talking for like a year but never did nothing sexual."

"Whatever . . . so you telling me that was the first time?"

She played with her fingers a little while looking at the floor. "Y . . . yes, it was."

Steve felt like his head was going to fall off if he had to listen to any more of this. He walked out of the bathroom as he said, "I don't believe you. This shit is crazy." He shook his head again, and walked downstairs to the kitchen. Angelia followed close behind him.

"I swear on my mom," she said when she got to the bottom of the stairs. "It's no reason for me to lie now. You caught me."

"Whatever, Angelia. I thought I could trust you. I really did. I should've known by you dealing with a bitch like Esha that you'd be on some kind of bullshit."

"What does that mean? I am nothing like her, not even close."

Steve didn't respond as he pulled a glass out of the cabinet, and got some orange juice from the fridge. He poured himself a glass and drank the whole thing. He then went through the cabinet silently for about a minute, and dug out a blender and a coffee maker. Then he asked, "Where the sandwich bags?"

"I reorganized yesterday. They in the drawer by the sink now."

CHAPTER
TWENTY

He found the bags in the drawer, pulled them out, and set them on the kitchen counter. He then grabbed a large pot, and filled it about halfway up with water. After turning the gas stove on a low setting, he set the pot over the burner, and walked up to the guest room without saying anything. Angelia followed right behind him.

"So that incident makes you feel like you can never trust me again?" she asked, standing in the doorway and watching what he was doing.

"I don't know . . . it's going to be hard to trust you, for sure," he said, as he pulled a full length mirror off the back of the door, and laid it on the floor to use as a table. He grabbed the duffle bag, and began pulling the kilos out, followed by the cut. He then started unwrapping one of the kilos of coke. As he removed each layer, the odor got stronger and stronger.

Angelia took a couple steps into the room, and watched what he was doing in amazement. "Where you get all that from? That's yours?" she asked.

"Yup," he replied, as only one layer was left on the first kilo. The odor was overpowering.

Angelia crouched down on the floor next to him to take a closer look. She wondered how he got that much, and who gave it to him. "Do you owe for that? Because you know I don't have the money to pay for that. We haven't even paid our rent."

"It will be paid tomorrow. Relax. I don't owe anyone that's going to come kill us or murder our whole family. It's okay. Relax."

"I was just asking. Can I just have a hug please? These last days you have been really torturing me, and I know I deserve it for what I did, but I love you and only you, Steve. I love you so much, and I don't know what to do."

Steve turned around and looked up at her. He stood up and held her in his arms for about 40 long seconds, while she cried on his chest.

"Please give me another chance. You can take my phone, put cameras in the house, or do whatever you want to do. I don't care. I don't want you to leave me, Steve."

The tears started to build up in his eyes, but he held them back, to appear strong. It hurt him more knowing what he did with Shila the other day, a girl that doesn't like or respect Angelia at all. He felt horrible. He was so in love with Angelia despite all the rumors people spread about her. At the end of the day, she was his baby, and he knew he had a lot to think about before he made any decisions. The last couple days, it had been easy for him to keep his mind off her by staying busy, but now that he was back in the house with her, all of the pain from the situation was coming back.

"We will see," he sniffled, wiping his eyes, and then got back down on the floor to remove the last layer from the first kilo. He set the whole thing on the mirror, and began to unwrap the cut mixture.

After removing all the layers from the cut, he set his scale on the mirror, and weighed out 10 grams of cut, then 5 grams of coke, just like his uncle told him. Angelia sat on the floor next to him, silently watching what he was doing. She started rubbing her arm, wondering if there was anything she could do to help.

"You hungry? You need me to do anything?"

"Naw, I'm cool. Thanks," he said as he threw everything in the small blender, and turned it on. He let it run for about a minute before opening it up and pouring it out. His trick was to always cut his dope in small portions, that way everything was mixed evenly. He never had any complaints about his product, so he wasn't going to change how he did it. This time he was a little nervous, since he had never been in control of cocaine this pure before, but he trusted his uncle's words and did what he said.

"So I'm changing my number today, and you can keep my phone. It won't be a lock on it. I'll delete my social media too, or you can have the passcodes to those as well."

It was irritating to Steve to hear her say these things. He never imagined he would have to do all this with her. She had really messed the trust up badly. "Okay, Angelia."

"Delete it?"

"Naw, you don't have to do that. Just the passcode is cool."

"Okay, I'll write it all down," she said, getting up and walking away feeling confident for the first time that she might be able to fix this situation.

Steve sighed again. He went back downstairs and pulled out some baking soda. He added only a few grams of it to the mix, then blended everything together for another minute. He then put everything into his Pyrex dish, then started to cook the dope up. He was curious to see how this dope would cook. After turning the coke to crack, he let it dry. Surprisingly everything turned out to be great. To him, it looked great. Now he was going to need someone to test it out for him, and he had just the guy in mind. He took a small piece of the rock to bring with him, and told Angelia that he'd be back in a little bit.

CHAPTER
TWENTY-ONE

Steve hopped in his car and drove about 10 miles away to visit a crackhead that he had known since he was a teenager. He was excited to see what this dude thought about it. When Steve pulled up and got out, he saw the guy looking out the front window, and he opened the front door by the time Steve got in the driveway.

"Hey, hey, uh, hey there, nephew. What brings you here so, uh, early in the morning?"

"I brought you a rock. Smoke this and let me know what you think."

"Okay, okay, okay, nephew. What I'ma owe you for it? You, you, you know I don't get my check for a couple weeks."

"You good. This on the house. I just wanna know what you think." He pulled out the rock and handed to him, and his eyes grew wide as he did a little dance.

"Oh, wow, nephew. This looks good. Let me get my pipe. Give me one second, and I'll tell you how it is, baby boy," he said, picking his pipe up off the table behind him. He put the rock in the end of it, and took a puff.

Steve watched him intensely, waiting to see his initial reaction. Within a few seconds, he started jumping around and yelling with joy. "Ouu, ouuu, ou, woo, woo, wooo! My eyes! My fingers! Yeah, yeah, yeah, YEAH!!!"

Steve saw all he needed to see, and turned around and walked out the door.

As Steve got in his car, the dude appeared in the doorway and yelled out, "I'ma holla at you when I get my check!" He closed the door, then Steve saw him appear in the window, waving at him with a huge smile on his face. Steve shook his head, smiled, and drove off. He knew he had some good shit. Steve turned up his radio, and started bobbing his head to Lil' Baby. Chills ran through his body as he thought about how much money was about to start flowing in. He turned the music up a little louder as he pulled back on the main street. Within a few seconds, he felt his phone vibrate in his pocket. It was a text from Shila.

Shila: Come get some head. My kids gone. I'm here alone.

He smiled at the thought, and sent a text back.

Steve: I'm on my way.

Shila: Yayyy! I was hoping you was back.

Steve: Got back early this morning. I'll be there in ten minutes.

Shila: See you soon.

Shila wasn't letting up on him, and had no intentions of slowing down. She was doing her best to show him how she felt. When Steve arrived, the garage was open, so he pulled in like last time, and went inside, closing the garage door behind him. She was standing right inside the door with a huge smile on her face, and she gave him a big hug before he had a chance to get all the way inside. "I missed you, baby," she said as she kissed him. She was wearing some red spandex shorts that were up her ass and a white tank top, looking sexy.

Before Steve got a chance to fully look her up and down, she dropped to her knees, and pushed him back against the door. She pulled his pants down to his ankles and grabbed his dick with one hand, and his balls with her other one. She slid the tip of his dick into her mouth, and sucked it slowly. His dick immediately grew to full size, and she started stroking and sucking.

"Gargh, gargh, gargh, gargh," she sounded off as his dick hit the back of her throat. She was going to town, wasting no time at all. She pulled his dick out of her mouth, and smacked it on the side of her face a few times before throwing it back in and going back to sucking like it was the Olympics of dick sucking going on and she was trying to get the gold medal.

"Shit, baby. Don't stop," Steve said, feeling his legs tensing up as he got close to cumming. "A little slower. Slower, baby, slower," he moaned and exploded inside her mouth within seconds. She kept her lips on his dick, sucking every last drop of cum out of him. His legs were feeling weak as he stopped cumming. He looked down at her and saw her kiss the tip of his dick.

She immediately stood up and said, "You liked that?" while looking up at him.

Steve bent over to pull up his pants then said, "Wow, loved it. Shit." He laughed and she smiled.

"Well, that's it. I hope you have a good day, baby," she said to him as she opened up the door.

He smiled as he got in his car and backed out the driveway. He was feeling great the whole way home with the radio up. He couldn't wait to get back home and get to work. When he walked in the kitchen, he had a huge smile on his face.

"What's the big smile for?" Angelia asked, looking down at his crotch.

"The dude loved the shit. It's really good, and I'm excited."

"What's that?" she said, pointing to his private area. "Why are you wet down there?"

Steve looked down and pulled on his pants, noticing a large wet spot that was very visible. "Huh? That? That's pee," he said nervously, then walked up the stairs.

"That's a lot of pee," she commented, following him up the stairs. "How did you manage to piss all over yourself?"

"Tryna piss in a bottle in the car. Shit didn't work as well as I hoped it would," he said with a laugh.

She was suspicious, but let it go. "Do you still need that pot down there on the stove?"

"Naw, I'm done with it," he said, crouching down on the floor to get back to work. He weighed out 10 grams of cocaine and 20 grams of cut this time, and put it in the blender. He turned it on, and started to weigh more out. After a minute, he turned the blender off, and heard a knock at the door. He got nervous and stood up.

"I'll get it," Angelia said.

Steve thought about who might be at the door, and soon he saw James coming up the stairs and into the room.

"Damn, nigga. Who you rob?" he asked.

Steve laughed. "Shit, nobody. Unk putting a nigga together."

"Damn, that's what's up. Why you not answering my calls? I thought something was wrong. You good?"

Steve looked at his phone and handed it to him. "Look, I ain't receive a call from you."

"Nigga, I called like 10 times. Check and see if you put me on block."

Steve looked at his phone and realized that James' number was on 'Do Not Disturb'.

"Damn, my bad. I must've did that when I was trying to put Angelia's ass on 'Do Not Disturb'. She kept blowing me up. What up, doe?"

"I ain't want nothing. I was just checking up on you and seeing what's good. I know you drove out of town, so I was wanting to make sure you got back alright."

"Oh, yeah. I got back earlier." Steve leaned a little closer to James and quietly said, "Close that door."

James walked and quietly closed the door, then sat down next to Steve on the floor.

"Bro, guess who I smashed?"

James laughed, but tried to stay quiet. "Nigga, nobody. Your scary ass."

Steve laughed. "Naw, naw, for real, take a guess."

"Stop playing, bro. How the hell would I guess that? Angelia? I mean, damn, it ain't like you have fucked anybody else in the last decade," he joked.

"Fuck you." They both laughed. Steve leaned in a little closer again and whispered, "Shila, dawg."

"Ewwwww, why?"

"Nigga, I don't know. I did it for my uncle. He wanted me to hit something new. He said it would be good for me," he whispered.

"And you picked her? You wild. Your uncle gone get you killed fucking her big mouth ass. If Angelia finds out, she gone kill you."

"No, she not. Shila ain't gone say shit. Why you ain't tell me the bitch had her shit together like that? I went by her crib. Nigga, she stay in them new cribs over there by the mall, bitch clean and all."

"I just said she be getting ran through and be with hood rats. She always been about her money though."

"Who ran through her?" Steve asked, pouring another 30 grams out from the blender into a pile.

"It's a few niggas I know that hit, and she got two baby daddy's."

"She ain't never let niggas run a train on her, has she?"

"Naw, naw. I ain't never heard that, naw."

"Nigga, the pussy was A-1. I ate that muthafucka," he whispered. "I tried to make her ass climb up the wall."

They both laughed.

"Nigga, you crazy, talking about you did it for your uncle. Nigga, your ass hurt. That's why you did it."

They laughed again.

"So, what's all this? Nigga, is that two kilos?" James asked.

"Nigga, it's about to be more than that."

"Angelia done brought the animal out your ass. You got a real bag and you fucking another chick. It's over. It's all over!" James said, giving him a pound. "My nigga said, you got him fucked up."

They both laughed.

"Naw, ain't no animal coming out."

"Bro, you literally changed overnight. The animal is out now. You wasn't like this last week, I'm trying to tell you!"

James noticed something different about Steve as he watched him work. He was focused, as if something new was motivating him. This made James happy and excited for him. Although James didn't mess with cocaine, he did grow weed, so he was happy that Steve was stepping his game up. He knew he had it in him, and he knew Steve was always smart and cautious about how he did things and who he did them with.

CHAPTER
TWENTY-TWO

"So, Shila had some good good?"

"Hell yeah, pussy and head were fire."

"Damn, I heard she was a little freak. I ain't think you would ever deal with a chick like that though, she kinda ghetto."

"She ain't that bad. It's probably the kinda chick I need. She seems like she loyal."

"Loyal as hell . . . just a slut when she single," James joked. "Her last baby daddy name Kev. Nigga, she was gone over him. Got the nigga two cars in her name when he came home from prison. She bought him all kind of Gucci fits, bought him a bag and everything. I'm talking like a couple bricks, she bought him. That nigga fucked it all up and fucked one of her friends. She put that nigga out," he said, laughing.

"Damn."

"How much of all that you gotta mix? I can help you. I got a couple hours before Eboni get off work."

"Nigga, I gotta do all this shit up. This will probably take me two days," Steve said, looking at everything in front of him. "I don't know, but then I'll need to compress it back together. Fuck! Damn, bro. I need to borrow about $1,200. I promise I'll pay you back tomorrow."

"I ain't worried about that. All this shit in here, I think you good for it," he joked.

"Yeah, i gotta buy a compressing machine. Niggas hate powder, so I'ma gone ahead and do this shit up right for them."

"Damn, that muthafucka cost $1,200?"

"$1,000, but it's worth it. It only compresses kilos though. I already got a little one, but I'm trying to remake everything into kilos, fuck it." They spent a couple hours joking around and mixing up the coke, then Steve followed James back to his house to get the money. After stopping by James' place, he drove straight to Detroit and bought the compression machine for $1,000. It was exactly what he was looking for, and after he put it in his back seat, he drove home, excited to press his first kilo with it.

When he came in the house, he saw Angelia lounging around. She had been laying around the house all day in her green Adidas track shorts that her ass filled out nicely. "You not hungry? I can cook," she said as she saw him set the machine down on the kitchen counter. He wasn't thinking about food though, he had money on his mind. Shila had sent him a few text messages telling him about some crypto currency she was investing in called Doge Coin that had doubled her money over night. She told him that he should invest in it, but he didn't know the first thing about it. He knew a little about Bitcoin, but he had told her that he would just talk to her later, because it sounded interesting.

"Order a pizza. That's bout all I got a taste for," he replied, picking up the machine to bring upstairs with him.

"That works for me too. I'll go ahead and order it," she said, getting up off the couch and grabbing her phone with one side of her shorts stuck in her ass.

Steve caught himself daydreaming as he stared at her ass, then he quickly had a flashback of another man enjoying it. He thought about how he had heard her screaming and calling for more. His face slowly turned sour. Finally, he thought about how she looked when he walked through that door and saw her, taking it from behind. It sent a chill down his spine. She had looked like something out of a porn video with her face all sweaty and her makeup all messed up. He couldn't remember the last time he had ever gotten her to look like that. Steve had always enjoyed making love to Angelia, instead of just having sex with her. He always thought she was beautiful, so he always like to look at her whenever he was inside her; he liked to hear the little signs and moans that came out of her as he went down on her. He loved feeling her heartbeat increase its tempo, and feeling her hands run down his back and body. He was never one to simply throw her around, pounding her to make her scream like a slut. He always treasured her like his baby, and even made love to her like so. And that was why seeing her with another man treating her rough like that, thrusting away at her like she was disposable, bothered him so much. Just the thought of it was pissing him off all over again. He wondered how long he would feel disgusted, and if he would now always look at her differently.

CHAPTER
TWENTY-THREE

When the pizza came, it was about 9 p.m. The doorbell rang, and about a minute later, Steve heard Angelia call him down to the kitchen. He showed up at the bottom of the stairs, and Angelia started giggling.

"What's so funny?" he asked.

"Look at yourself. You are covered in coke."

Steve looked down at himself. His arms, shirt, legs, and hands had coke all over them. Steve smiled. "Yeah, I guess I do look ridiculous."

"Why you not using gloves with that stuff?"

"Shit, I should be. I will get some."

"You gone mess around and be a whole crackhead," she joked, but Steve didn't see the humor in her comment.

"You get some ranch?" he asked.

"Yes, sir. I did not forget your ranch." She walked to the other side of the counter and grabbed it for him.

"Thank you," he said, standing at the island and pulling a big slice of pizza out of the box.

"You welcome," she replied, getting a slice for herself.

They walked over to the couch with their plates and started to eat. She ate slowly, mostly watching him as he ate. He was putting particular effort into not looking at her. He was, in a way, uncomfortable with the way she was staring at him. Deep down, they both knew that things between them were severely damaged now. It wasn't the first time they'd watched each other's mouths as they ate like that, yet somehow, he couldn't bring himself to watch her. He didn't want to watch her at all. He didn't want her watching him either. The last thing he wanted at the moment was some fake, forced conversation or intimacy between them, and it seemed like that was the only thing Angelia was committing to doing. He hoped she would just give him some space, but she didn't want space. She wanted to get him back into her arms as soon as she possibly could.

"So, I was thinking about applying for some remote jobs, you know the work from home type stuff."

Steve did a little nod with his head. "Yeah, that's cool," he said, remembering when he told her to do that. He wasn't even sure how to feel about the fact that it had to take all of what had happened for Angelia to start actually taking his feelings and thoughts seriously. The more he thought about it, the more it annoyed him.

"I been filling out apps. They say they hiring, so we'll see. My mom called today. She asked about you."

Steve finally looked up at her. "You tell her what you did to me?"

Angelia made a face, and hesitated before she said, "Ummm, no. That's not her business."

"That's too bad," he replied, taking another bite of pizza and looking away. "You shoulda seen what she had to say about it."

"I'm grown. I'm not interested about what she has to say about it. They have enough to talk about over there. That's all Mexican's do, and I didn't think we needed their input."

Steve could hear that he was starting to hit a nerve.

"So you told your mom?" she asked.

"Naw, I haven't talked to her in a few days, but I was thinking about it."

"Why?"

"Why not?"

"I just think that's stupid to do, especially since we are working it out."

Steve stopped chewing and looked at her. "Working it out?"

Angelia lowered her voice and said, "I mean . . . yeah . . . aren't we?"

Steve went back to chewing, set his piece of pizza down, and just stared at it for awhile. "I said I'll see what's going to happen. Everything is weird now."

Angelia sighed, then took another deep breath, knowing that he was right. She wished they could just skip ahead a month or two and get past all of the awkwardness. "I know. It sucks for me. I think I'm going to drink myself to sleep tonight."

Steve shrugged but didn't say anything. After a long pause he said, "Sucks for me too."

"I'm sorry, Steve. I really am. And I just want to show you that I'm willing to work this out and do whatever it take to earn your trust back," she said, watching to see if what she said caused any kind of reaction in him. He maintained a relatively apathetic look on his face though, and just seemed to keep staring at his pizza or off into space. Angelia couldn't bear to watch anymore. She got up to fix herself a glass of Ciroc.

Steve watched her out of the corner of his eye as she got up and walked to get a bottle. He shook his head. She was the one that had caused this problem, and now she was going to get drunk over it. He hadn't seen her drunk in years, and he was definitely not in a mood to deal with 'Drunk Angelia' tonight, because he had a lot of work to do, and when she would get drunk, she was the definition of counter-productivity. Soon, a text came through from Shila.

Shila: Where do you see yourself in 5 years, sweetie?

CHAPTER
TWENTY-FOUR

He stared at the text while Angelia poured a drink. When he glanced up, he saw her standing at the island already sipping from her glass. She thought Steve was planning to get up to go back upstairs to work, but now she saw him pause to look at his phone. She was curious as to who might have sent him something.

Steve could tell that she was watching him. He decided to play it cool, and pretend like he wasn't doing anything out of the ordinary. He texted Shila back.

Steve: I want to save up and maybe start my own business so I can work for myself.

Shila: That sounds good. I could see you being a boss. What kind of business you want to start?

"Who is that?" Angelia's voice came from the kitchen rather sharply. He didn't want her to think anything was wrong, so he kept the text open as though he had nothing to hide. He looked up at Angelia with a particularly uninterested face once again.

"Why? What's up?"

Angelia shrugged. "Just asking. You look pretty serious over there. Is everything okay?"

He looked back at the phone quickly, stared at it for a while, and then laughed as another text notification went off.

"Yeah. Everything is cool. James is silly."

"You told him about what happened with us?"

"Naaah," he said, falling back comfortably on the couch. He went back to thinking about what kind of business he could see himself owning. It had been a long time since someone had asked him that kind of question. The people he was surrounded by on a daily basis weren't into starting businesses, so whenever he brought up the topic, they had nothing to add. They were willing to listen, but never asked him any specifics.

Steve: I'm not sure yet. Something that makes a lot of money.

Shila: Lol I hear you, but you need to know what field you want to go into and be serious about following through.

Steve: You right. I'm going to start thinking seriously about it.

Shila: Good idea.

Steve: What about you?

Shila: I see myself owning more dump trucks, probably about 3 more.

Steve: You have a dump truck business?

Shila: Yes, going on 4 years now.

Steve: What made you get into that?

Shila: My dad was doing it before he died. He left me two dump trucks and since then I've added another one.

Steve: Wow, that's pretty cool. Is it good money?

Shila: $700 a day per truck, so I think so.

Steve's eyes grew wide. He knew that there was money in what he was doing, but $700 a day of legal money for every truck out there wasn't a joke either. He texted her back.

Steve: Lol that's crazy. I need to see what kind of dump trucks these are. You may have to help me start my company. I ain't know you was into all that.

Shila: I told you, let me upgrade you. Lol a lot of people don't know I own trucks. I don't even tell people because they all haters anyways.

Steve nodded approvingly. He was starting to see that she was a woman who knew how to make moves and get her money up.

Steve: Damn, that's good. I'm serious, I need help with setting up a company and some more shit.

Shila: I got you, baby. I already told you, I'ma make you mine.

Steve smiled to himself. He wiped it off his face almost immediately after, and then checked to see if Angelia was still looking at him. She wasn't. He maintained a straight face as he went back to texting.

Steve: Lol smh.

Shila: What you shaking your head for?

Steve: Because you crazy, cute, and smart at the same time.

Angelia looked up at Steve again. She was tired of watching him fully absorbed into his messages, so she walked out of the kitchen with her drink and an attitude. Steve watched her walk out, then looked back at his phone.

Shila: Thank you . . . I think Lol.

Steve: What you about to do?

Shila: Lay in my bed alone and think about how good you ate my pussy. Dream and fantasize about that.

Steve: Oh yeah. It felt that good?

Shila: Yes, sir, my pussy getting wet thinking about it.

Steve: Don't make me pull up and eat that muthafucka right now.

Shila: I'm about to sit on the kitchen counter and wait for you.

Steve: 20 minutes Lol.

Shila: Okay Lol.

CHAPTER
TWENTY-FIVE

He was dirty and hadn't been in the shower all day, but he was about to go pull up on her before he went back to work. It wasn't too long of a drive, and he had all night to work. He went into the bathroom and washed his hands and arms off, changed his shirt, and left the house. He drove straight there, and the garage was open when he pulled up, so he pulled in and parked. The moment he turned his car off, he received a text message.

Shila: I'm on the counter waiting, just come in. The door unlocked, don't forget to put the garage down.

He smiled as he got out of the car and pushed the button to shut the garage door. When he came inside, there was only a dim light on. It smelled fresh and clean inside, like always. He walked around the corner into the kitchen and saw her sitting on the granite island counter top, with a black silk robe on. She had her legs open, ready for him. He walked across the hardwood floor and when he got close, she grabbed his head and mashed his face into her pussy. He went right to work licking and sucking her pussy like it was his favorite smoothie. "Oh, baby, yes!" she moaned as she laid all the way back with her legs spread wide. He moved up to her clit and started licking it round and around. "Oh, my . . . God . . . you gonna make me cum!"she screamed as she became more and more into what he was doing while he made slurping sounds over and over again. Then, she felt him spit on it. "I'ma cum. Don't stop, baby please!"

He gripped her ass cheeks and licked around in a circle while he had her lifted slightly in the air.

"Baaaaaby, I'm cumming!" she screamed, shaking uncontrollable. "Ouuuu, baby, ouuuu!" she said in between heavy breaths and finally he slowed down, licking softly and gently sucking her juices up, admiring how pretty her pussy lips looked. He noticed some cream between her lips, which he licked up with his tongue, then he kissed her lips before he backed up. She was limp, holding her titties and trying to catch her breath.

He was starting to like making her cum. Watching her eyes roll and legs shake as she leaked out juices of pleasure turned him on. This was an experience he already enjoyed with Angelia, but now that he was messing with Shila, he couldn't deny that getting this reaction out of her did something for him too. He believed strongly that the best way to get a woman to keep wanting you was to make her orgasm, and so far, he had never been wrong about that. Licking the creamy cum from Shila's pussy and kissing her to have her taste a little bit of her own orgasmic essence were the things that he got hard off. It made him feel like she wanted him completely, no matter what he did or wanted to do.

"Okay, boo. I gotta go," he said, smiling and wiping his mouth. Shila looked at him with hearts in her eyes as he turned around and walked out the door.

"Lock the door!" she yelled as he closed the door. She was still laying on the counter, not wanting to move.

Steve went back home to find Angelia dancing, holding her glass in her hand, and singing a Selena song. He walked past her and went upstairs to take a shower. He stared at himself in the mirror for a while, and as he did, he couldn't help but think about Shila. Perhaps he was more heartless than he thought he was. As he was getting naked, Shila sent him a text.

Shila: You are amazing!

He smiled and sent an emoji, blowing a kiss, then jumped in the shower. He was in there for about 10 minutes washing up before Angelia busted in the door, a little clumsily.

"Why you ain't asked me if I wanted to shower with you?" Steve could detect a little tremor in her voice, a tremor that usually only appeared when Angelia was either drunk or well on her way there. He poked his head out of the shower curtain and took a quick look at her. He could see it all in her eyes.

"Stop playing. Get your drunk ass out of here," he said, knowing she was tipsy. He shut the shower curtain on her completely. Within a few seconds, she snatched it back open.

"I'll rip this curtain off. I can look at you."

He shook his head trying to hold his laughter back. He knew she was only drinking to build up some courage to mess with him.

"Can I get in?"

"Naw, I'm about to be out in like 5 seconds."

She rolled her eyes, and walked out of the bathroom dramatically closing the door behind her. He went back to taking his time as the hot water poured over his athletic body, that he had kept in pretty good shape since high school. He thought about Angelia for a second, but Shila kept replacing that thought. She was on top of things and stayed on his mind, helping him to keep from being too stressed about Angelia.

CHAPTER
TWENTY-SIX

Once he stepped out of the shower, he got dressed. There was still a bunch of work for him to do. When he got back into the guest room, he looked at the mountain of cocaine he had created. He sat down, and went back to mixing 30 grams at a time.

"You want a drink?" Angelia asked, walking into the room behind him.

"Sure. Put a little juice in it for me," he told her as he turned the blender on. Another text came through from Shila.

Shila: Goodnight handsome. Talk to you soon.

Steve: Goodnight sexy.

Soon, Angelia came back with his drink. "Thanks," he said as he took it from her and took a sip.

"You welcome. You want some help? I can separate some of it for you."

"Yeah, just make 20 gram piles of this, then 10 gram piles of this, and I'll do the blending. I'ma go grab a few more of these coffee bean grinders, because the blades are already getting dull on this one. I can tell by the different shades of white."

"I can grab them for you. I have to go to the grocery store anyway. I'll try to have them before you wake up . . . looks like you got a lot to do. This is a lot."

"Not yet," he said with a smile. "It will be when I finish."

"I know I never told you this, but I remember when I was thirteen, my dad used to make me and my three brothers walk across the Mexico border over here to the U.S. with a kilo right here like under my breast and one strapped to my back. We would all walk across like every two weeks."

"Kilos? Of cocaine?"

"Yes."

"Damn, that's crazy. Why y'all stop?"

"My mom threatened to leave him because he already had a lot of money and hadn't been caught. She felt like he was begging to get in trouble by continuing to do it, so she said she was going to leave him if he didn't stop. So he stopped and invested in real estate."

"Oh, wow. You still have family over there?"

"Yes, of course. Everybody is still over there. All my brothers got deported because they got caught smuggling here. They tried to do their own thing when my dad stopped."

"I been dealing with you all this time and you ain't never told me about that. Why?"

"I was embarrassed, honestly. I hate talking about it. I still have cousins, aunts, and uncles in California that are a part of stuff, but I haven't seen them in forever. They hit me up on Facebook sometimes, but that's about it."

"When I get rid of all this, you can call they ass up. Tell them you need them thangs," Steve said, joking as he took a drink.

She giggled. "I will. I'll call them, and they will be so happy. I just couldn't tell my mom or dad or they would be pissed. They don't want me around that lifestyle anymore. That's why we all the way up in Michigan."

"So, it's safe to say, I been fucking with the plug daughter."

She giggled again. "Most definitely. I am not even kidding. My dad used to have kilos taller than you in our kitchen, stacks and stacks. I mean, hundreds of them when I was a little girl. I know his ass still loaded with money. I just don't like asking him for nothing because he would tear off into my ass."

"So your dad was in a cartel?"

"Yes. Please don't tell anyone I'm telling you this, but yes. He had to do a lot and pay a lot just to get out. They didn't want him to stop. It was crazy, but yes, he was in there. They used to have shit on planes, ships, and all that stuff."

"Damn, your dad don't even seem like he was doing all that. He all calm and chill . . . always working."

"Yeah, until someone pisses him off," she said, weighing out another 20 gram pile and setting it off to the side. "I'm going to get you some masks and gloves too. This stuff is strong."

"Bet. I was gonna grab some, so that's cool."

They continued until he was at one whole kilo. After they had it together, they set up the machine, then compressed it all together. He planned to leave it in the machine overnight so it could be hard as a rock. He set alarms on his phone every hour, so he could get up and apply more pressure to it. "Are you sleeping in the bed tonight? It's stuff everywhere in here and I know you not going to clean it up tonight."

"Yeah, I guess," he said, walking downstairs to get another slice of pizza.

She followed behind him to fix herself another drink. Suddenly, Steve came to a sudden halt. He thought he heard footsteps. He looked back at Angelia for a moment, and was completely silent. Angelia, at first, didn't understand what he seemed so concerned about, and then she heard the footsteps herself. The steps were coming quickly from the other side of the door, and getting louder. Steve didn't have any time to react.

CHAPTER
TWENTY-SEVEN

BOOM! Three guys came through the door, kicking it open. Steve, on reflex, jumped in front of Angelia to protect her. The three guys that were now in front of them were not there for her though. They were there for Steve. At first, he thought that he should fight them until he saw one of them with a gun drawn. He knew that reckless moves could very well cost him his life, so he dropped the idea. The guys went straight for Steve, rushing him and taking him to the ground.

"Stop! Oh, my God!" Angelia screamed, running and jumping on one of their backs as he was kicking Steve who was now laying on the floor. All three men continued to attack Steve mercilessly.

"Nigga, I don't ever forget a face!" one of the men yelled as he kicked Steve in the head.

Steve, curled up on the floor to try and shield himself from the kicking and punching, removed his arm from his face and took a quick look at the man who had just spoken. It was the same guy he caught Angelia in bed with. The same guy he punched in the face in the parking lot of the restaurant the other day.

Steve was still staring at him when he pulled out his gun and pointed it at his face. Jon Jon took pleasure in the terrified look on Steve's face, tormenting him with the idea that he might die at any moment. Steve's life was in his hands, and that's exactly what he wanted. After he saw the horror in his eyes, Jon Jon decided to give him a taste of real pain. As he took the gun from being pointed at his face to his leg, he couldn't help but smirk. He stood there, just smiling at Steve's fear for what seemed like an eternity to Steve.

POW! A shot rang out, and the blistering hot bullet tore into Steve's thigh.

"Bitch ass nigga," Jon Jon said calmly, happy to watch Steve grab at the bullet wound in agony. Steve couldn't even scream. The instantaneous pain was like nothing he had ever felt before. His mouth opened, and his whole face went tight, but no sound came out. After a second or two, it started to settle in, and it was a hot, searing, horrible feeling that left him in total shock. When that feeling set in, Steve let out a groan. He could feel the pain, but there was nothing he could do to protect himself or retaliate. They were all over him. He simply laid there, bleeding on the kitchen floor while holding his leg.

Angelia couldn't believe that Steve had just been shot. "Jon Jon! Please don't kill him!" she screamed as one of the guys held her back with his arm around her neck in a choke hold while she kicked, trying to get loose. Jon Jon paid no attention to the words that came from her mouth. This was between him and Steve.

"Check the house for money and drugs and let's get out of here," Jon Jon instructed.

"You really about to rob us? Really!" she screamed, but he once again acted like he wasn't able to hear her.

One of the guys ran upstairs into the main bedroom. He flipped the mattress, then started pulling all the drawers out of the dressers. He found nothing that seemed to be worth taking, so he moved to the next room. When he opened the door to the other room, the first thing he noticed was the black duffle bag on the floor. He paused for a moment as his eyes moved to the large mirror on the floor. He grabbed everything he saw and ran back downstairs. "Come on! I got something."

The other guy threw Angelia to the ground and within a minute, they were out of the house.

"Are you okay?" Angelia said, gasping and rushing over to Steve's side. He was bleeding from the mouth and the leg.

"Yeah. Fuck, they took the dope, didn't they?"

"Yes. Was that everything?" she asked, thinking about what would happen if they weren't able to pay the rent and Steve wasn't able to pay his debt.

"Yes, I think so. Arggh!" he growled, holding his leg.

Angelia was confused. She knew that something else must have happened between Steve and Jon Jon for him to come to their house and attack him like this. She wanted to know what exactly went down, but at the moment, she had something else to do. "No! No! What the fuck did you do to him?" she shouted, her voice trailing off as she ran up the stairs. She got shoes, her gun, and her car keys and was back downstairs. She tossed Steve his cellphones and told him she would be back as she ran out the door.

CHAPTER
TWENTY-EIGHT

Although the pain was severe, he couldn't tell what hurt worse, the pain or the amount of money that just ran out the door. Angelia jumped in her car, shaking and fumbling with her keys to start it up. Adrenaline rushed through her body, and she could barely think clearly. She backed out of the driveway and peeled out, hoping that her idea of where Jon Jon and his boys were going might be correct. She sped down street after street, cornering hard, and accelerating as quickly as she could until she hit the main road. She hit the main road and her eyes raced around, trying to find Jon Jon's car. There was no traffic at all though, and the first three lights she passed were green. Finally, she saw a red light in the distance, and she planned to race through it until she recognized the car in the left turn lane. It was a black BMW 6 series 4 door with the blinker on. Knowing that this was Jon Jon's other car, she smashed the pedal to the floor, and accelerated to 45, 50, 55 until . . . SMASH! She drove right into the passenger side of the BMW, deploying its airbags, and sending both of the cars spinning into the middle of the intersection.

By the time Angelia came back to reality, she had a loud ringing in her ears, and all she could hear was the sound of her breathing. The airbag had smacked her in the face, but the adrenaline was still flooding her body, so she got out and ran up to Jon Jon's car with her gun, slowing down once she got close, ready to shoot anyone that made a sudden move. Both of the passenger windows were smashed, and as she walked around the back of the car to the driver's side, she could see all three of them slumped over, not moving. She opened the back door on the driver's side, and took the duffle bag. She walked quickly back toward her totaled car, but noticing its condition, she kept walking past it back in the direction of her house. She quickly got on the phone to call an Uber, then she called the police to report her car stolen. After she got done making the police report, she called Steve, and the Uber was pulling up. "Where the fuck did you go, bitch! I'm shot!"

"Shut up! You not going to die. Did you call the police?"

"No."

"I'm on the way back now. I'll take you to the hospital when I get there," she said, hanging up the phone and jumping in the Uber.

When she got back to the house, Steve had already managed to get himself up off the floor. He was sitting in a chair at the kitchen table with his t-shirt tied around his leg. She walked right past him without saying a word, and put the duffle bag and the gun in their bedroom. She grabbed the keys to his car, and ran down the stairs.

"Let's go, my car totaled," she said, holding out her hand and helping him to his feet.

He was a little bewildered at how fast Angelia had confidently taken control of the situation, so he just went with her. He was helpless in his current state by himself.

"So you officially crazy," he said, as she sat him in the passenger seat of his Impala. The door slammed.

"Why you say that?" she asked, starting up the car.

"You crashed into them niggas. You coulda killed them."

"They coulda killed you when they shot you. Are you ready to tell me why the fuck he came back and shot you?"

Steve knew she wouldn't let it go. This was the tenth time she asked the same question. "Since you can't stop asking, I seen the nigga in Detroit, and I knocked his ass out."

"What you mean you seen him in Detroit? Just randomly y'all was in the same place at the same time, and you went at him?"

"Yeah."

"Bullshit. Tell me the truth, Steve."

"That's the truth. I seen him, and didn't think he noticed me, so I knocked his ass out and left."

"Where was y'all at?"

"Some restaurant."

"You know we have to move now, right? It's not over. That nigga crazy as fuck, so I hope you can make some money because I'm not going to continue to sleep in that house."

"Fuck him! I got shooters too. I'm not worried about them niggas. I'll have that nigga dead by next week. Fuck you mean? Talking to me like this nigga don't bleed like I bleed."

CHAPTER
TWENTY-NINE

She was silent. She knew Steve never failed her when it came to protecting her and keeping her safe. "You find another place just to be safe, but I'll handle that nigga when the time come. He better just gone about his business and leave me alone, or he gone have a problem he don't wanna have. And you better leave him the fuck alone as well!"

Angelia made a face. "That was over that day. Don't start with me!" She stared ahead at the road, trying to focus on driving. They droved in silence for a few minutes.

"That was some gangsta shit you did though, I gotta admit," Steve said, playfully hitting her arm.

Angelia did all she could to keep a straight face. "Whatever."

"For real, that's all I was thinking about when he shot me. I'm like, fuck they gone get all my shit," he said, laughing.

She shook her head. "You wasn't thinking like, they gone kill me . . . just they about to take my drugs?"

He burst out laughing. "I knew he wasn't gone kill me. I'm surprised he shot me at all. That nigga shot me quick too, but it felt like he was standing there pointing at me forever with that gun. But I ain't think he was gone kill me."

"Well, I did. I didn't know what the hell happened. It scared the shit out of me, then they didn't have on any masks or nothing like they didn't give a fuck that you would know who it was."

"Soon as I seen him, I'm like damn. I thought they was about to fuck me up. My ribs are sore from them kicking the shit outta me, and my mouth was bleeding a little, that's all. I mean, yeah, he shot me too, but it ain't shit. You smashed into them niggas!" he said, laughing. "That's more serious than what they did. Them niggas some hoes anyway. I hope all three of them niggas retarded now."

Angelia giggled. "You are silly. The way I was feeling, if I wouldn't have seen them on the road, I was going to drive my car through his house. I was getting my baby's shit back by any means!"

Steve cracked up. "Shut your little pretty, prissy ass up!"

"I'm little, but I'll tear some shit up! I don't care about nothing when I get mad."

"I can see that," he said, still laughing to himself. "My baby said, give our fucking bag back now!"

Angelia giggled. "I was bout to shoot his ass too."

Steve laughed. "Hell naw!"

"I'm so serious."

"I know. That's why I'm laughing so hard. You caught they ass. Damn, that's so crazy."

"I woulda looked all night," she said, looking over at Steve with a smile.

Steve laughed and shook his head.

"Wait a second," Angelia continued. "Awwww. Did you call me your baby? Am I your baby again?"

"Yeaaaah, you made up for that. I still want your phone, Facebook password, and we getting cameras in the house and all that," he joked. "I'm kidding, but naw, we okay. You my baby for sure." He leaned over and kissed her on the lips, but the pressure he put on his leg made him reel back in pain. The kiss sent butterflies through her stomach, and she got the chills. Her eyes were starting to water, but she wasn't going to let a tear fall. She rolled down the window, then glanced over at Steve.

"Your leg alright?" she asked.

"Yeah, I just sat on it when I leaned over to kiss you."

"Okay," she said, placing her hand on his. "You gone be alright." She couldn't help but allow a big smile to come across her face. She had her baby back. Although what she did was chaotic, she couldn't be happier about making the crazy decision to get their stuff back.

CHAPTER
THIRTY

The next morning, they packed up all their clothes and important stuff. Steve's leg was all wrapped up and he had a slight limp. They left all the furniture behind. Angelia had to do most of the work, but she didn't care. She moved as fast as she could, packing the car with bags. James' uncle had a house for rent for them that was nice and in a better neighborhood in Pontiac, on the north side. They went there once James dropped off the first and last month's rent to his uncle for them.

When they walked in, they felt immediately at home. The house had a warm, welcoming vibe, and it felt so calm and peaceful in there. It smelled like fresh paint and Pinesol. Everything was brand new looking, or whoever was in there before them was incredibly clean.

"I like it," she said, looking around at the kitchen and setting a few bags down.

"Me too, and we got an attached garage, so that's cool too. The place is nice, and I can't wait to settle in, but we got work to do, baby. I need to make some bricks up and then go sell this shit," he said.

"How about just sell the one in the machine first, get some money, then you can come back and I'll help you. We will knock it all out. It's a kilo in the press machine that they hadn't even took that's ready to go."

"Oh yeah, sure is. That's a good idea. I'm about to pull up on some niggas right now then. Start separating the shit into piles again on the counter, just like last time, and I'll be back in a lil' bit."

"Okay." Angelia started to get the scales and everything set up on the counter, while Steve grabbed the kilo and hobbled out of the house. She looked at him in admiration as she saw his determination to make money and do what he had to do.

When Steve hit the road, he called Juice.

"What up doe, bro!" Juice answered.

"Shit, where you at? I'm tryna pull up on you and show you something."

"Same spot I seen you at last time. I got two houses on that street. Come through, and you'll see me when you pull up."

"Okay, bout 10 minutes and I'll be there."

Steve pulled up and walked inside the house with a backpack.

"What you got, lil' bro?" Juice asked, standing by the big round wood table.

Steve took off his backpack and set it on the table. He unzipped it and pulled out the kilo of cocaine inside a Ziploc bag. He set it down on the table in front of Juice and said, "Some good coke. Check that shit out."

"Damn, this bitch look good," Juice said as he grabbed it and looked at it through the bag. He opened it up and broke off a corner. "Oh yeah, this that shit. Damn, this muthafucka ain't even stamped. You mind if I drop it in the water? If it's right, I'll cash you out for this right now. You got some more?"

"Go ahead and do what you wanna do. Yeah, I got some more."

"Skee!" Juice yelled out. "Come look at this shit! Nigga, this shit got that glaze look all through it." His homeboy came in from the living room and took a look for himself.

"Shit, how much you want for this?" Skee asked.

"I'm already buying this muthafucka. Back up," Juice joked.

"You got some more?"

"Pipe down. You doing too much," Juice said, and they all started laughing. "Nigga out here just stepping all over a nigga toes," Juice said quietly while turning on the stove.

"Well, what you call me in here for if you wasn't gone show me no love?"

"Awwww, here this nigga go with this mushy shit."

All of them broke out laughing again.

"I'ma let you get down. No worries. Bro, how much you want for this though?" Juice asked once again.

"I'll tell you once you cook it and it come back."

"Lil' bro, this coming back for sure. I'm cooking to see how much more gone come back. I know good dope when I see it. This better than the shit I'm getting right now, and I got the best shit around here right now."

"They high right now, but you can get it for $43,000," Steve said as his back was sweating.

"$43,000?" Juice asked, looking back at him while he was locking it up in the Pyrex. "Bring me every single one you got. I want all of them."

"Greedy ass nigga!" Skee said.

They laughed.

"Nigga, I'm paying $45,000 right now. Hell yeah I want all of them. And this shit better. You can sit right here while I run through your whole bag. I'm bouta give you $43,000 right now though as soon as I finish with this," Juice said as he started doing a two-step dance. "I'm bout to murder these niggas with this shit right here boy!"

CHAPTER
THIRTY-ONE

Steve was excited to see Juice's response. This was the biggest sale he had ever made. When Juice went upstairs and came back down with a duffle bag and started laying big stacks of money on the table in front of Steve, it nearly made his dick hard.

"Ten thousand, count that. Twenty thousand, thirty thousand, forty thousand," he said as he put each stack down. "And three thousand right here." He had a lot of 20 and 50 dollar bills.

"See, my money gone be all hundreds. You ain't gone have to count all that bullshit," Skee said, making fun of Juice.

Steve and Juice both laughed.

"Fuck you. I coulda gave him all hundreds too. This just what I had on hand, that's all. You want all hundreds next time?"

Steve laughed. "Yeah, to make it easier."

"Say less. I got you lil' bro. I promise you it's all there. I'm like a money counting machine myself," he joked.

"Count your shit and take your time. This nigga always short," Skee said jokingly. They all laughed while Steve counted the remainder of the bills. He quickly realized that this was the most cash he ever had all at once. As he counted the last few bills out, he was so happy he wanted to run all the way home with his backpack, but he held his composure as if he was used to it.

"It's $43,000 on the nose."

"When can you bring another one through?"

"Probably going to be tomorrow. I'll call my people and set something up."

"Lil' bro, don't give this shit to nobody else. Nobody. I'll buy all of them. If you need more money, let me know. I want them all."

"Naw, naw, I got you. I'ma just holla at you for sure. I don't be dealing with these niggas out here like that."

"Alright, bet. As soon as you get them, bring them through. I'ma have your cash on hand."

"Okay, cool," Steve said before putting the stacks into the backpack and walking toward the door. Juice noticed him limping as he walked away. He wondered why he hadn't noticed it when Steve came in.

"Why you limping?" Juice asked.

"I got shot on some bullshit," Steve said, walking out the door with Juice coming right behind him. He got in his car and sat down with the driver's door open to talk to Juice.

"Damn, everything straight though? You know I got them killas if you need me."

Steve laughed. "Yeah, everything cool."

"For real, let me know if you got any issues out there. I got your back on whatever."

"Okay, fasho," he said, giving Juice a pound then closing the door. He pulled away with a huge smile on his face, trying his hardest to contain his excitement. He called James right away and told him to pick up some blenders and to meet him at the house. When he got back, Angelia was still working at the kitchen counter, so he threw the bag on the floor.

"Hey, come count this for me, Angelia." When she unzipped the backpack, her eyes grew wide. A huge smile was plastered across her face while she pulled the stacks of money out. That was exactly the reaction Steve was looking forward to seeing.

"You sold all of it?" she asked, staring at the stacks of money in front of her.

"Yep. One nigga. Gone," he replied with a nod. "And he want some more. James is on his way over to help right now. Count that up, then you can go house shopping for the crib. How much do you think you need?"

Angelia looked at Steve, then glanced up at the ceiling while she did a little dance with her finger as if she was adding it all up in her head. "I should be good with about $8,000."

"You can start with $8,000, but if you need more, no worries. Get us a king size bed though this time. You come back with some queen size bullshit, you ain't never shopping again," he joked, while texting Shila to get some ideas on a good store to get furniture from.

"Where you planning on going?"

"Value City."

As soon as she said that, Shila's response came through.

Shila: Art Van.

"Go to Art Van," Steve told her.

"Okay, I will."

Steve told her to count out $8,000, which she did happily. After getting a few things together, she left to go shopping. After she was out the door, he went right back to work. He started adding 22 grams of cut to 10 grams of coke instead of the 20 to 10 he was doing before. About a half hour later, James came through the door.

"What up, bro?" James said, taking a spot next to Steve at the counter.

"Shit, just getting this next one together. That first one gone," he said, glancing at James with a grin on his face.

"For real? Hell yeah! So you adding 22 grams of cut this time? Why you switching it up?"

"Because the two extra grams ain't gone hurt it at all. That shit jumping back so good no one will know the difference. Make sure you blend each batch of that shit for a little over a minute."

"Okay, I got you. So with two extra grams, what you gone get extra out the whole kilo?"

"Only like a little over 2 ounces. Something like that."

"And how much was you getting per ounce?" James asked curiously.

"Bout $1,200 or something like that."

"Damn, that's an extra almost $3,000 you gone get off each kilo. Sheesh, bro!"

"You feel me?" Steve said, laughing and starting up the blender.

"You about to make me jump in and get some of this money," he joked.

"Nigga, Eboni will kick your ass!"

They both laughed.

"Hell yeah she would. She ain't into that shit at all."

"What we need to do is buy you some more grow lights. Do you think your basement still got enough space left?"

"Plenty of space. I mean, shit, what you wanna do? I been thinking about it, but just ain't had the money to drop on the new lights yet. I was gonna run through two more harvests then upgrade my lights and give myself some more square footage to grow in down there, you feel me?"

"Oh, fasho. Well, I got the $3,500 you fronted me for your uncle right here. What you gone need on top of that to get set up how you want it?"

"I'll add a thousand to that. That's all me and Eboni got extra to our name right now. I only fronted that cash to you because it's you, but that's our last, bro. For me to get the basement how I'd like it to be, it's gone be about $10,000," James said, turning off the blender.

"Alright, alright. If I put up the $10,000, how much can I get? You cashing in every three months?"

"If you give me $10,000, I can produce every two months and can give you $10,000 every two months if that's cool?"

"I'll take that. When you want to start?"

"Whenever you get the money."

"Grab it out that duffle bag right there. Count $10,000, and get what you need," Steve told him.

James leaned back a little and smiled at him. "Stop playing," he said as he walked over to the bag. He unzipped it and nodded his head approvingly.

"Nigga, you turning up out here. Angelia about to be sucking your dick from the back, bro."

Steve laughed. "Nigga, she was already doing that."

They both laughed.

CHAPTER
THIRTY-TWO

James counted out $10,000 and was excited. "Maaaaan, I love you. We about to turn up!" he said, setting the cash to the side and getting back to refilling the blender. Over the next two hours, they worked together and got the next kilo done. They were laughing and joking around so much that the time flew by. Steve liked having someone there to help him make the time go by faster. After gathering it all together and weighing it out, they threw it into the press and went back to work on mixing up some more, only taking a break to tighten down the press after an hour. An hour after that, they had another one ready to go. After another hour and a half, another one was done, and then another.

James had to go home now, but he had saved Steve a ton of time by helping him out. Steve was almost done with the last kilo when Angelia came back home with plenty of bags from Target and Walmart. She had towels, silverware, glasses, plates, food, sheets, pillows, bathroom decor, kitchen decor, and much more. She brought every bag in and set them all next to each other in the living room.

"I'm sooooo tired," she said as she collapsed on the floor next to the bags. "The furniture will be delivered tomorrow. I got everything we need for the living room and the bedroom. I came out pretty good so far."

"Okay, cool, cool. Sounds good to me. We got a lot done over here too."

"Y'all been working all day?"

"Yep. He literally just left like 5 minutes before you came through the door. I'm on the last kilo right now, then I just gotta put each one in the machine to make it hard, but I know what I'ma do to speed that process up. I'ma put some Acetone on it."

She giggled. "My dad used to do that sometimes too."

"I'm starving. Did you eat yet?" he asked.

"No. I can go get something for you if you want me to."

"What you got a taste for?"

"Coney Island will work for me. I'm just ready to light some candles and soak in a nice hot bubble bath. You joining me? You know we have a big tub in here now," she said, sucking her teeth.

"I seen that. I just might have to. It's definitely a celebration. We bout to get some money out here."

"Ayeeee!" she yelled as she got up, doing a little twerk dance. "I'm just playing. What you want from the Coney?"

"Corn beef sandwich and fries. That sounds so good to me right now."

"Yeah, it do to me too. Okay, I'll be back," she said, grabbing her purse and leaving through the garage door.

Steve looked at his phones. He had been ignoring them all day. Shila had sent two text messages earlier.

Shila: Hey boo.

Shila: Where you been all day?

He read them and finally replied.

Steve: I was in the hospital.

Shila: Are you okay. What happened?

Steve: Yeah, I'm good. I got shot.

His phone immediately started ringing, and he answered. "What happened? Why you get shot?"

He laughed. "I don't know. I guess the nigga wanted to shoot me," he joked. "Naw, I got into it with a nigga and he shot me in my leg. I'm all good though."

"Wow, that's messed up. Can you walk still?"

"Yeah, the bullet went right through, so no biggie."

"Oh, good. Damn, I want to take care of you," she whined. "Is she keeping your bandages clean and rubbing you down?"

He laughed. "Damn, that sounds good. And naw, not really. I been trying to get stuff done all day. I should probably take a break."

"See that's why you need somebody like me, so I can take good care of you. Be your head doctor and everything. See if you can get away. You can come over here for a couple days with me and recover. I promise I'll treat you right if you can come by."

Steve looked around briefly at the bags on the living room floor, the powder all over the kitchen counter, and the kilos ready for the press. "Nah, that ain't gone work right now. I just moved, so I can't, but I do appreciate the offer."

"Well, I miss you so much. I can't wait until I can see you again. I just took some pictures for you. I'm going to send them in a minute."

He laughed. "Okay. I'ma get back to work. I'll hit you up later."

"Okay, handsome. Byeeeee."

CHAPTER
THIRTY-THREE

Steve started cleaning up a little bit, and his mind started to wonder about how long he could keep all this up. He was getting back to a good place with Angelia, but he had been hitting it off with Shila lately. He put all the remaining coke and cut away, then sprayed down the counter and started to wipe it off when he felt his phone vibrate. Two pictures of Shila came through, each of them in different lingerie sets. She was showing her sexy body off. Her light skin looked so good to him in the first deep red set, and then the second aqua set looked just as good. He pressed 'love' to all her pictures, then she sent a picture of her pussy. It was perfectly shaven, and looked delicious to him. He started to think about how he'd love to get a taste of it right now, but his leg was sore, and it was already 10 o'clock. All of the work he had been doing finally was catching up with him, and he felt tired. It had been a long day, but he was happy with all he had gotten done. He sat at the kitchen table and made a to do list for tomorrow while he waited on Angelia. Only a few moments later, she came walking through the door with the food.

When she sat the bag down on the table, the smell of the food made his mouth water. Angelia went to get some napkins and drinks, but by the time she turned around, he was done with his sandwich. He had finished it in what seemed to be three bites.

"Dang, Papi. You ate that quick. You must've been hungry," she said, handing him a napkin.

He wiped off his mouth and replied, "Hell yeah. That was good. Thanks."

"I'm going to start a bubble bath for us right now. By the time I'm done eating, it should be ready."

"Okay, cool. I'ma go brush my teeth and then take a look through these bags to find something to sleep in since we have to sleep on this hard floor tonight."

"Nope. We don't," she said with a big grin. "I bought a queen blow up bed that's in that box over there. I got sheets and everything for it. I wasn't going to let you sleep on the floor with your leg like that. And I'll change your bandages in just a second."

Steve raised his eyebrows and nodded approvingly. He was impressed. She seemed to be really on top of things now.

"Okay, bet. I see you," he joked.

"You know I got you, boo."

Esha called her, but she didn't answer. She was planning on giving her a call back tomorrow. Once she was finished eating, she brushed her teeth, and then proceeded to change Steve's bandages and gently clean the wound.

"Ouch," Steve said, as he winced a little in pain.

"Did that hurt? I'm so sorry," she said, gently dabbing the gunshot wound with cleaner. "I'll be gentle."

"Nah, it's fine. You're doing great. It feels better with your hands on it."

Angelia blushed. "How long do you think it'll take before it's completely healed?"

Steve shrugged. "Well, the doctors didn't really say, but I'd guess it'll be a few weeks, at least. I mean, the bullet went straight through. That's a good thing, but it also means there's an entire hole in my leg for my body to heal up. I'm glad it didn't hit my femur and shatter that shit though. That woulda been real bad."

Angelia nodded. She added some ointment to the wound, and began applying fresh bandages. "Well, I'll be here to help you change and dress it until it's all completely healed. You don't have to worry about that."

Steve smiled at her and tilted his head.

"Are you a little queasy from all the blood and stuff? You look like you scared."

"I ain't scared of blood. Steve, I bleed every month. Besides, it's really not that bad. I've seen worse wounds back in the day with my father."

"For real?"

"Guys used to be over there with their entire arms and legs freshly chopped off. I seen it all. This just a bullet wound, so it don't bother me none."

After she finished dressing the wound, she gestured to Steve to go get his bubble bath. Steve took a peek into the bathroom, only to see candles lit all around the tub. It was a deep, whirlpool tub that was pretty big, almost like a jacuzzi. She had the water filled with bubbles to the top, and a cloud of steam rose above the water, and coated the mirrors and she dimmed the light. There wasn't a shower curtain yet, but it would work for now. Before they got in, Steve took out the blow up bed, and blew it up.

"Awww, baby. I woulda did it," Angelia said, seeing him laying down the last pillow.

"I know, but you was doing other stuff. No biggie. You ready?"

"Yes, here you go." She poured him a glass of Dusse mixed with Coca Cola.

"You on top of things tonight, I see. This just what I needed," he said as he finished the whole glass.

She giggled. "You was supposed to sip that with me!" she said, gently smacking his arm.

"Oh?" he said, giving her a smile before getting undressed and walking out of the bedroom toward the bathroom. He had stripped all the way down to his birthday suit, and Angelia lustfully watched him walk out of the room. He was in a pretty good mood for someone who had recently been shot. He was glad to finally have his hands on some real money. It almost felt like a dream, and he didn't want to wake up. He had missed Angelia so much, and he was excited to be spending quality time with her. He never knew that she would go so hard and be damn near ready to die for him like she did. He felt like he was special again to her, and he also felt like he was a lucky man.

He rested his hand on the tub, and slowly dipped the foot of his wounded leg into the water. It was steaming hot, but it felt good as he lowered his body into it. He took a seat, stretched out, and laid back and cleared his mind, focusing on the moment, which made him feel good inside. There were no worries.

CHAPTER
THIRTY-FOUR

Soon, Angelia came walking inside. She stopped right by the sink and took a sip of her glass of liquor before slowly stripping off her clothes. Steve admired her perfect, curvy silhouette as she removed her bra seductively. Her breasts sat up perfectly. She slowly removed her underwear from her round hips and ass. They were perfect, just how Steve liked it. She walked over slowly and got in slowly, taking her time to get used to the temperature of the water.

"Ouuu, it's nice and hot," she said, slowly bending at the knee to lower herself in.

"Yeah, it feels so good. I needed this," Steve replied, splashing some of the water on his face.

"Me too," she said as she sat down, placing herself directly in between his legs. She loved how much bigger he was than her. She was able to slide right up against him, backing up just enough to feel his soft penis press against her back. She had missed this closeness so much. She leaned her head back against him and began rubbing his legs gently.

"I feel so good, baby," she said.

He wrapped his arms around her. "Me too, baby," he replied, kissing the side of her face.

"I've missed you a lot, you know."

"What parts of me?"

She started playing with Steve's fingers as he embraced her. "I've missed your kisses for one."

"How much?" he whispered into her ears.

"A lot," she responded quietly.

Steve squeezed her body gently. "Show me."

"Show you?" she asked as she twisted around on all fours to face him, and kissed him softly once, then again, and again. Then she licked both of his lips and gave him a smile. "You taste just like liquor."

He smiled and she pecked his lips again then got the towel and began washing his chest, arms, neck, and back.

"Stand up," she told him, putting more soap on the towel to wash his lower body.

He slowly stood up out of the water, and his dick was hanging in her face, almost touching her forehead. She grabbed his dick with one hand and began to wash it with the towel with the other one. Then she lifted it up, and started washing his balls before asking him, "You want me to get your ass too?"

He laughed, "Naw, I'll get that in a sec."

After rinsing his dick off, she put it in her mouth and began stroking it slowly. She was never able to fit the whole thing into her mouth, but she definitely gave it her best effort. She had missed him so much, she was trying to swallow it. After getting him fully hard, she backed off a little, and started rubbing her hands up and down his body. Soon, she started bathing herself, covering her whole body up with soap, washing every part of herself. Steve sat down and watched her. She then sat back down while he washed her back.

"Baby, I want you so bad right now. Meet me in the room when you finish in here," she said as she got up slowly, and backed her ass up right in front of his face. He surprisingly grabbed her by her ass and stuck his tongue between her cheeks and licked it. She turned to look back at him. "I'll be waiting," she said as she stepped out of the tub.

He bathed himself one more time with the towel, then pulled the drain on the tub. The water began to rush down, and he stood up and turned on the shower. Angelia came running back into the shower with him and they splashed water at each other as they rinsed off. They were both laughing as they were drying themselves off. When Angelia bent over to dry her legs, Steve smacked her ass, making a loud sound and causing it to jiggle. She smiled at him and shook her head.

"Ass so phat," he said, hanging his towel up on the towel rack.

"It's all yours, baby. Come here." She pulled him close to her and he kissed her passionately. He had missed her so much he couldn't take his lips off of her. From her lips, he moved to her neck, where her tender spot was, then he made his way down to her titties. As he engulfed one of her nipples in his mouth, she screamed out, "Ohh, baby! I missed you!"

Steve was starting to get lost in her body. He knew Angelia got hornier whenever he played with her neck, so he went back to work on it. He traced his tongue from her tits back to her neck, and then started massaging her tits with his hand. He could hear her quietly moaning as he worked on her neck, and she held his head to her neck, letting him know not to stop. With his lips and tongue still on her neck, he raised his hand and put one of his fingers into her mouth. She licked it thoroughly until it was dripping wet. He then used his wet finger to gently rub and stimulate her nipples. He could feel them hardening against the tip of his fingers.

Her heart began to beat faster and faster, as her breathing increased. She could feel her pussy getting wetter and wetter by the second. Steve then started to suck on her breasts again. He sucked on each one, not neglecting either one.

Angelia pushed him back.

CHAPTER
THIRTY-FIVE

"Your leg, baby. You need a break from standing. Come in the room." She hopped down from the sink and took him by the hand. She walked him slowly over to the blow up bed and laid down. It was dark in the room, but they could still see each other perfectly. She spread her legs, licked her fingers, and then rubbed her pussy lips gently, maintaining eye contact with Steve. He smiled at her. She withdrew her fingers and gestured for him to come to her. He soon dove his face between her legs, licking her in all the right ways. He knew her body so well. He knew exactly how to lick, spit, and suck on her clit while fingering her pussy to make her cum quickly.

"Yes, papi," she said, grabbing the back of his head while both of her legs spread back in the air. Within minutes she yelled out, "I'm cumming, papi!" She exploded, while rubbing her clit aggressively. He pushed her legs back further, and gently licked her asshole with his tongue. Seconds later, he moved his tongue around her asshole until he had it so wet that his tongue dipped in and out with ease, which caused her to shake uncontrollably. The intensity of the orgasm, followed by the sensation of him licking her ass had her feeling incredible.

"Yessss! Lick my asshole, papi!" she moaned, spreading her ass cheeks for him. He started tongue fucking her in the ass, repeatedly spitting on it then stroking at it again with his tongue. "I'm cumming again, papi. I'm . . . ouuu, I'm cumming!" she moaned while she rubbed her clit faster until waves of ecstasy began to pulse through her body as she felt him sucking up her juices like a vacuum cleaner. The sensation made her back up a little, screaming, "Ouu, papi! My God! Hold on, wait!" She pushed his head back from her.

"Okay, okay, okay. I'll be gentle," he told her as he stuck his face back in her pussy and slowly tongue kissed it softly, barely sucking on her. "Turn over, baby," he instructed her to lay on her stomach with her ass tooted up a little. He stretched out on the floor and licked all between her ass with his wet tongue. He went up and down until he saw her gripping the sheet.

"Yes, Papi! You licking my ass so good. I love you!" she moaned. "Yesss!" He stuck his thumb in her pussy while his finger massaged her clit and his tongue licked all around her asshole. "Papiiiii! Ouuuu! I'm . . . oh, you making me cuummmm!" Her body tensed up tightly as she exploded once more and he started to suck up her juices again. She was shaking every time his tongue touched a certain part of her pussy. "Papi! Damn!" she said as she flipped over and got up. "Now, you lay down."

He did what she said without hesitation, and she immediately began sucking and licking his balls, slobbing all around his dick, trying to fit as much of it into her throat as she could until she gagged. He was hard as a rock and she was sucking him aggressively, but she didn't want him to cum in her mouth. She wanted all of his cum inside her. After his dick was dripping wet, she stroked the length of it a few times, then climbed on top of him and slowly slid his dick inside her. She let out a deep exhale as it filled up her insides. She arched her back a little and rested her arms gently on his chest, maintaining heavy eye contact with him as she started riding him nice and slowly. She slowly sped up her tempo gradually until the tip of his dick was hitting a particular spot inside her. A minute later, she came again and collapsed on top of him.

"Shit, Papi! I can't stop cumming." Her pussy was leaking. Steve had her so turned on. The juices and tightness of her pussy continued to grip his dick until he felt his dick twitching as it squeezed the cum right out of him.

"Shit, baby. I love you, baby," he told her as he pulled her down and kissed her with his tongue, grabbing her ass with one hand and moving her up and down on his dick.

"Baby, this pussy feel so good," he whispered not even an inch from her lips. Their lips stayed close to each other while she worked her hips in a small circular motion. "I'm bout to cum in this pussy again, baby," he whispered, and she kissed him with her tongue.

"Cum in it, Papi," she whispered, moaning seductively, still working his dick with her pussy. She rode him slowly for a few more minutes and soon she felt his dick getting harder and harder. She increased her tempo faster and faster.

"I'm bouta cum," he whispered, gripping her ass and sticking his dick further and further until it felt like there was something stopping it, and then he exploded inside her again. This one made him completely weak. He lost all the strength in his hands and legs, and had to use Angelia's body for support. She received him completely, holding him as close to her body as she could while he emptied himself inside of her.

Steve was so in love with Angelia, and her pussy that he didn't think there was anything that could provide a better feeling. Sex with Shila was great, and her pussy was one of the prettiest and most enticing he had ever seen, but there was still something about Angelia that he couldn't bring himself to forsake. Her pussy was so addictive. He had been having sex with her for a long time, and each time he did, it felt just as good as the first time. He loved the way it squeezed and pulsated against his penis. He loved the way it gripped his penis, from the base all the way to the tip. And he most especially loved cumming inside her over and over again. He could never use a condom with her again. Nothing beat the feeling of his thin skin touching her warm, delicately soft insides. Cumming in her never got old.

Steve looked at Angelia, and started to run his fingers gently through her hair. She fell asleep on top of him, and they remained that way, naked and tightly embraced, all night long. They didn't wake up until 9:30 the following morning, when both of their cell phones were going off. Finally, Angelia, being the first to wake up, picked up her phone and sent it to voicemail.

"Papi, get up," she quietly spoke into Steve's ear.

CHAPTER
THIRTY-SIX

Steve groaned at first. He had barely heard what she said, and didn't pay much attention to her. She tapped him gently but rapidly on the chest until his eyes opened a little bit wider.

"Papiiii! Come on, get up."

"Whyyyy?" he groaned again as he rolled over to face the other side of the bed.

"Your phone keeps ringing, and you have to put another kilo in the machine."

Steve paused and kept his eyes open. She was right. He did still have work to do. He wished he could stay in bed a bit longer.

"Okay, I'm getting up in one second," he said as he shut his eyes briefly and sighed.

Angelia smiled at him lovingly, then she laid back down and texted her mom. After she texted her mom, she sent a text to Esha.

Angelia: What's up, hoe?

Esha: You bitch! What you doing? You busy?

Angelia: Yes, been fucking all night girl. Still laying in bed.

Esha: Get it girl. Wow, you put Jon Jon in the hospital.

Angelia: Noooo, you got to stop by but I heard about it. My car got stolen.

Esha understood Angelia didn't want to text any details over her phone.

Esha: He's okay though. We should go and see him. He asked about you. My brothers had a talk with him because he was talking crazy about you so y'all need to talk.

Angelia: Okay, when?

Esha: Today we can meet up and go up there.

Angelia: Okay, that's cool.

Esha: Next question . . .

Angelia: What!

Esha: Lol, come to Cali with me. It's me, Jon Jon and his brother. You HAVE to come with me. I need you and Jon Jon wants you to come.

Angelia: After I talk to him, maybe.

Esha: What you gone tell Steve?

Angelia: I'll think of something. We back rocking.

Esha: Awww, that's cute.

Angelia looked over at Steve one more time as he laid in bed with his back turned to her, breathing gently. He had fallen back into a light sleep. She moved a bit closer to him and started rubbing his back.

They didn't' stay in bed for too much longer. By the time he got up fully, Angelia was already in the bathroom getting ready to leave. He knew their phones had been going off all morning so he was sure she had shit to do as well. He took a bath after Angelia and got dressed. His plan was to go see Juice with two kilos.

While he was on his way there, the seriousness of how quickly the money was going to be coming in set in for Steve on the drive. It was about 10 o'clock in the morning when he got there.

"What up, bro?" Juice said, excited to see him. "Man, they love that shit you gave me last time. I hope this the same."

Steve dropped his backpack on the table and unzipped it.

"Should be. It do look a little tanner, but I don't think nothing changed." He pulled them out and Juice examined them. He only had to look at them for a few seconds before nodding approvingly.

"Naw, this that shit still for sure! Hell yeah, bro." Juice had $86,000 laid out in all hundreds for Steve. "He pointed to the stacks and said, "Should be an easy count for you this time."

Steve nodded and took a seat at the table. He counted up the bills, and everything was right. After he packed the money away, he looked up at Juice and said, "I can bring you two more later if you want them."

Juice's eyes lit up. "What? Hell yeah, I want them! What time can you bring them by?"

"Shit, in a few hours."

"Perfect. It might not be all hundreds, but it's gone be $86,000."

Steve shrugged. "All this shit spend the same, so that's cool with me."

"Damn right. This shit fire though, bro, and it's a good price. Niggas taxing out here. We can take over this bitch if you stay consistent."

"I think my dude running low. He said he had like three and a quarter kilos left or something like that."

"Nigga, get it all if you can. I can give you $45,000 for each one. No problem. I need them bad, all of them."

Steve laughed. "Okay, I got you."

"For real, bro. Don't sell it to nobody else."

"I'm not. I got you fasho."

"Say no more."

Steve picked up his backpack and gave Juice a pound before heading out the door.

When he sat down in his car seat, he got chills down his spine. He couldn't believe he had another $86,000 in the car with him. He tried to contain his excitement to the best of his ability. As he drove away, he turned his music up, and started drumming happily on the steering wheel. When he pulled out on the main road, he started laughing and sped away.

"Fuck with me!" he shouted, looking at himself in the rearview mirror. At this rate, it wasn't going to be long before his whole life was changed. There was an unexplainable joy that was overtaking his whole being. Everything was going perfectly for once.

CHAPTER
THIRTY-SEVEN

As soon as he got back home, he sat down at his kitchen table to recount the money he got from Juice again. It was all there. "I'ma need a money counter in a minute," he mumbled to himself as he packed the money back away in the bag. Angelia was still home when he got back there. She had thought about leaving and just sending him a text message, but she decided to stick around until he got home so she could talk to him.

"I'm going to Cali this weekend to visit family," she said, kissing him as he got to the top of the stairs. "I wanna go grab something to wear for while I'm down there."

"This weekend? For how long?"

"Just two days. Me and Esha both gone go together. I'ma go see some of my family and she's doing the same. That way, if you need them for something, I'll have easier access to them after going to visit," she said, smiling at him and pecking him on the lips.

Steve thought for a moment then said, "The only thing I don't like is who you going with, but be safe." Steve reached in his backpack and counted out some money for her. "Here. Go buy you something nice." He wrapped the bills in a rubber band and tossed it to her. She caught it excitedly. "That's about $2,000. Have fun."

"I love you, Papi," she said with a big grin on her face looking down at the money. She ran over to him and kissed his cheek twice before kissing him once on the lips. She then started to get ready to meet up with Esha, and left the house soon after.

James came over a couple hours later to pick Steve up since Angelia had the car. Together, they went to meet Juice at his house for the second time today.

Steve walked in and took out three kilos and put them on the table. "This about 12 more ounces too."

"I want it all, bro." Juice was happy, and had the stacks of money all ready for Steve again. "James, you gone have to help count some of this too, bruh bruh!" Juice said, pointing at him.

"That's what I'm here for." He smiled, grabbing a stack of hundreds.

"How much you gone charge me for the 12 ounces?"

"$1,250 a piece."

"Bet, so about $15,000 more. That should be $135,000 right there. Let me grab 15 more right quick." He ran up the stairs and came back with a stack of hundreds. Steve nodded as Juice set the stack down in front of him.

Angelia got in the Range Rover with Esha. There was a lot of giggling and teasing between them before any real conversations ever began. Angelia and Esha always had something to laugh about, even when the topic wasn't particularly funny. They could basically see each other walking towards one another on opposite sides of the road, and they'd start laughing until they locked themselves in a tight embrace. Perhaps, it was weird to other people who got to witness it, but they were like two peas in a pod. Steve never really understood what the hell was wrong with them with all the giggling and laughing they were always doing. For Angelia, Esha helped her let go, forget her troubles, and filled her life with laughter and fun.

"So you been at home trying to be wifey again, huh?" Esha joked.

"Shut up," Angelia said, smiling at her.

"So what the hell happened?" Esha asked, turning her radio down so she could pay attention.

Angelia quickly made a face then tried to summarize all of the important details. "Jon Jon came to the house and kicked the door in. Him and two other dudes came running in, and they shot Steve."

Esha was a bit taken back. "What! He ain't say all that." She faced forward and frowned. "What the fuck wrong with him?"

"Girl, Steve seen him in Detroit and knocked him out so he came back for him, shot him, and took some dope. I'm like aww hell naw. That's all we got."

Esha's eyes grew wide from getting the gist of it. "So what did you do?"

"Girl, I jumped in my car and went looking for his ass. When I seen him, I crashed my shit right into his ass, then jumped out and took the dope back."

Esha stared wide eyed at Angelia while she told her story, then bust out in laughter. Esha was hitting her steering wheel, laughing and screaming. "That's why you my bitch! Nigga, don't ever think about robbing us!"

"Right!" Angelia screamed in agreement.

"Okay, okay," Esha said as she calmed down and took a few breaths. "He ain't tell me all that. You fucked them up though. One of them broke they arm and his face got all scraped up from the airbags. The other two had concussions and I think one of them broke a leg. He was talking hella shit like he was bout to do something to you so I called my brother and he hashed that shit out with him."

CHAPTER
THIRTY-EIGHT

After about 20 minutes, they arrived at the hospital. They went through the front glass revolving doors, and took the elevator up to the 5th floor. They walked down the hallway and found his room number. When they walked into the room, Jon Jon smiled a little when he saw them.

"Your ass ain't got it all," he said as Angelia approached his bed. She walked up to him and hugged him as sincerely and gently as she could. She rubbed his arm gently, trying to express some kind of remorse for his current condition.

"I didn't mean to do you like this, you know. But you was doing too much and -."

"Say less. Say less," he interrupted, dismissing her reasons. "I was tripping, coming into your shit and taking all y'all shit. I coulda caught that nigga in the streets like he caught me, so I apologize to you. You forgive me?"

"Yeah, I forgive you. I apologize too," she replied, wrapping her hands around his, making sure to be careful around the I.V. that was dripping fluids into his vein.

"Awww, y'all kinda cute," Esha said.

"Shut up," Angelia said, turning around and giving Esha narrow eyes. She stood up and sat beside Jon Jon on the side of the bed.

"This nigga was talking about killing your ass. His car is totaled too. You coulda killed them. You crazy. I'm like okay, this too serious. I had to call my brother. Tell her what you was saying, Jon Jon."

They laughed.

"I'm like, your girl dead. I'm killing that bitch. She like, noooo!" he laughed. "But your brother was right. Shit got sloppy, so it's all good. I'ma take that. Me and your boyfriend still got issues, but I'ma keep you out of it."

"You the one crazy, and you talking about me," Angelia said, shaking her head.

"So we are all going to Cali this week, getting a bomb ass AirBnB and turning up. Fuck all that bullshit. We living it up and having fun this weekend," Esha said.

"I'll be ready. What you gone do with that arm?" Angelia asked.

"I'll be alright. You know this arm ain't got nothing to do with how I put this dick on yo' ass."

The girls both laughed.

"Zaammmmm, I hear that," Esha said.

"Ouuuu," Angelia joked.

"Don't even pack. I got some Chanel shit for you too. I hope your dude don't get too mad at you."

Angelia smiled. "I'll handle that, no worries. Let's focus on me and you, like before."

"You got it."

"Alright, we leaving with your Ray J looking ass," Esha joked. "Don't he look like Ray J?"

"No! My baby look better!"

Steve had just got to James' house. He wanted to show Steve his grow setup he had just built. He had put up new walls in his basement, and ran the electrical for new lighting all through there. He was excited and so was Steve, although Steve didn't know too much about growing weed. James, on the other hand, was nearly obsessed with it. Ever since he got started growing, he was reading books about it, searching the internet, and talking to every grower he could meet about different techniques and methods for growing. He had a few harvests under his belt now, and he was starting to really dial in on the drying and curing process. With his new setup, it would be much easier for him to manage the temperatures, air exchange, and humidity levels, and he'd have more wattage and even more lighting over his canopy, so his yields should be going up significantly.

Steve was happy to listen to his friend, but he was more interested in the money that could come out of the endeavor. After they were done looking around, James took him to send $8,000 to his uncle's account, then took him back home.

When Steve got settled back at home, he laid out all his money, and counted out $100,000 for his uncle. He didn't forget the agreement that came with his uncle plugging him. After he set his uncle's money aside, he counted out another $100,000 for the Texas plug his uncle had told him about. Steve then pulled out his phone to call his cousin Sabrina, Swift's daughter.

"Heeeeeyyyyy, cuzzzz!!!" she answered in a loud, high-pitched voice filled with excitement. Steve knew Sabrina was always happy to talk to him, even though they didn't talk to each other as often as they would like. Sabrina was always fun to have around, and Steve was always happy to hear her voice.

"What up? What you doing?"

"Nothing much. I actually just got off work." She sighed exasperatedly. "I'm also kind of hungry, but I don't know what I have a taste for. Don't you hate that?"

He laughed. "Yeah, I know how that feels." He glanced over at a clock on the wall to check the time, then got back to Sabrina. "Shit, I was just calling because your dad said something about how he wanted me to link up with you. I'm not sure if he told you or not."

"Hmmm, hmmhm," Sabrina confirmed. "Yeah, he called me and told me. Where you at?"

"I'm at home on the north side. I'll text you the address."

"Okay. I can come now. I'm just right here in Auburn Hills wandering around."

"Okay, pull up. I just moved here yesterday so my furniture isn't here yet. It's supposed to come today, but we will see."

"That's cool. I'm not judging. I'll be there in a little bit."

CHAPTER
THIRTY-NINE

Steve hung up and looked around. Somehow, he had thought Angelia had cleaned the place up a little bit more than it looked. Apparently not. He got up and tried to clean up a little, putting particular emphasis on making sure his money was put away and there was no drug paraphernalia or residue sitting out. Back when he was sorting out his uncle's cash, he made sure to give him all the big bills so it would be as small and portable as possible.

Steve was just finishing up wiping down the counter tops with cleaner when Sabrina arrived. She pulled up in a silver Mercedes with a blue top. The coupe was so big it could have been a four door. She stepped out, carrying her Louie bag in her hand and dressed to impress. Steve watched her from the window as she approached. She never fell short when it came to dressing. They hugged each other tightly as soon as she walked through the door.

"Heyyy! How you been?"

"Good. How about you? You pulling up looking like a real boss lady," Steve said, giving her a nod.

"I'm trying, I'm trying."

Steve showed her around his new place a little, then walked her over to the counter where he had Swift's money laid out. It was arranged carefully and neatly, all of the bills lined up next to each other in perfect rows.

"I gave you all hundreds, so it should fit right in that bag you got."

"Yes, it looks like it will fit without a problem. I don't need to count it, do I?"

Steve shrugged. "If you want to you can, but it's a hundred grand right there. I counted it four times, but you should probably count it again just to be safe."

Sabrina sat down and started counting the bills. Steve was surprised at how quickly she counted up the money, running it through her fingers like a professional. She was done in no time. It was like she was a human money counter herself.

"Yep. $100,000," she said, placing the stacks neatly into her bag. "I'll let him know that I got it. When the next time you going to see him?"

"I'ma go up there tomorrow and holla at him."

"Oh, cool. Well, it was good seeing you, cousin. I guess I'll get going."

"Great seeing you, Sabrina," he replied.

"We really need to get out more too. I always have a blast when I'm with you. Let's spend some time together. We should go out to eat sometime soon. Oh, and I like your house too. It's nice."

"Thanks. And yeah, we will put something together soon. How that sound?"

"Sounds great," she replied, heading for the door.

Sabrina was soon out the door, walking gracefully back to her car. Steve watched her back out and drive away. Twenty minutes after she left, he was resting his legs looking through his phone when Angelia texted him and told him that the furniture place had called to tell her that the delivery drivers should be arriving in the next 10 minutes. Steve let out a sigh. He was just getting comfortable, and he had to get up again.

Almost exactly ten minutes later, the doorbell rang. The furniture company arrived, and asked Steve where he wanted everything. Steve didn't have to do anything to help because they brought enough people to bring everything in and assemble it all. As they were setting it all up, Steve noticed that the five piece bedroom set was a little too big for the room, but the crew found a way to make it work, and he was happy with how it all looked once it was in place. As he saw his new furniture in place, his mind instantly thought about the type of house Shila had. He wanted to have something like that, newly built with a lot of space. Compared to how she was styling, his place wasn't anything special. At the same time, where he was at now was a big step up from where he came from.

Steve walked around his place again, and couldn't help but think that he really wanted something bigger. This would work for now, but it was going to be temporary. Angelia did a nice job selecting the furniture. For the living room, she got two tan colored sofas with three matching glass tables, two end tables and a coffee table. A buzz and a ping from his phone interrupted his thoughts. He pulled it out to see a message from Shila and smiled to himself. It was always crazy how Shila seemed to reach out to him while he was thinking about her. He dropped back on the couch to focus on his conversation with her.

CHAPTER
FORTY

Shila: Hey boo.

Steve: Hey, sexy. I was just thinking about you.

Shila: I felt you Lol.

Steve smiled to himself.

Steve: Lol clearly. What you doing?

Shila: Just got home. I'm about to get the kids in the tub and ready for bed.

Steve: How was your day?

Shila: Great. What about yours? And what was you thinking before I texted you?

Steve: Mine been good. I was thinking about the dump truck thing.

Shila: Oh, what about it?

Steve: I want to do something with it, get involved, you know? How much money will I need up front to start?

Shila: It depends what kind of truck you want. Let's meet tomorrow. I'll show you what kind of trucks I have.

Steve: Good idea. Okay, we can do that. Does about 5 or so work for you?

Shila: Yeah, that's perfect for me.

Steve was excited. He had driven by large trucks before, but never really taken an up close look at them. Although he was nervous about doing something that was completely new to him, he felt confident being in the hands of someone who knew the business well and knew about the trucks he would need. She had already explained that she had been in the business for a while, so he trusted her judgment. The way he and Shila had been moving, he was sure that he could trust her to walk him through it, or at least get him started and show him the ropes. He figured he could learn everything else as time went on. If he were to get into it without a mentor, it might be too risky for him, but he never did things that way. He always made sure that everything was lined up the way it should be before he made a move. Doing it any other way never made sense to him. Another text soon came through on his phone.

Shila: Come get your dick sucked and them balls licked.

Steve laughed. She was so bold, but he liked it. He thought about going to see her, but a guilty feeling came over him since everything was back in order with him and Angelia. They had made love the other night, and he was going to do his best to be a faithful boyfriend. He wanted to make things work, but he wasn't sure how to tell Shila the news. He figured he would tell her tomorrow face to face when they met up instead of over the phone.

Steve: Damn, that sounds tempting, but not tonight.

Shila: Okay.

He then dialed his mom's number. He hadn't talked to her in almost a week now which was probably the longest time he had gone without talking to her all year.

"Hello," she answered.

"Hey, momma. What you doing?"

"Oh, nothing. Just cleaning up and listening to the news. This pandemic has been crazy. Make sure you are wearing your mask out there."

"I have been," he lied. His mom was always watching the news and getting scared and anxious afterwards. She was the type of lady that went out and bought all of the water and toilet paper once she heard there might be a shortage. She was always telling Steve how the world was going to end soon and that he needed to get closer to the Lord. Although he loved her a lot, he had a hard time engaging with her in her 'end times' way of thinking. She was mixed, but acted more white than anything. Steve had more of the opinion that if the world ended, then it ended. There was no point in focusing energy on things outside his control, so he tried to stay positive about everything.

"That's good. When you coming to see me?"

Steve hated going over there. She stayed in a trailer park in Auburn Hills, but it wasn't the nicest of places. Plus, her trailer wasn't that big and she had been paying on it for what seemed like forever. "I was thinking this week, maybe Friday. I have a lot to do tomorrow, but I'll come through Friday. I can take you to look at some nice trailers."

"I'm fine with the trailer I have now. I'm not moving, and I don't have the money to move even if I wanted to."

"I didn't say anything about you buying it. I'm buying you a new one in a better area."

"Oh . . . well, son, that is very sweet of you. I would love that, and I know exactly where a better one is. It's in Auburn Hills, and it's a beautiful area. It has schools and a park across the street. Oh, Steve, it's gorgeous. You're going to love it!" Steve could hear her excitement building and that made him happy.

"I can't wait to see it. You can call tomorrow and get the price and all that. Tell them you are going to be putting $15,000 down on whatever one you want to get. I'll pay the rest of it off soon too, so you don't need to worry about what the payments are. I just want you to be happy and in a nicer area."

"Steve, honey, you're the best. I'm going to cry." Her voice got shaky and the sound of it brought tears to his eyes. "I love you, son. Thank you so much, baby. Thank you!"

"You welcome, mom. You know I got you always."

"I . . . I know . . . son. I'm . . . just so happy, I don't know what to say."

He smiled as a tear fell from each of his eyes. "Okay, Ma. I'll talk to you tomorrow, okay?" he replied, tearing up a little more and trying to get off the phone.

"Okay, son. I love you, baby."

"Love you too."

CHAPTER
FORTY-ONE

Steve hung up and cried tears of joy for a few minutes. Just the other week, he was struggling to pay his rent, and now he was setting his mom up in a nice, new place. The feeling he had from being able to put his mom in a better position was priceless to him. He couldn't believe how quickly things were changing for him. As he wiped away a few of his tears, Angelia came walking through the door. "You know they only trying to give me $1,800 for my car? That's not even enough to buy a new one." She was frustrated and had an attitude.

"No worries. You will get something soon. Just use mine. I thought you was going shopping. Where is your bags?"

"These stores don't have nothing. I think I'ma just shop in California instead."

"Oh, that would be cool. Good idea."

"I missed you though," she said, kissing him on the lips. "How do you like the furniture I picked?" She started walking up the stairs.

"Good job. You did good."

"Thanks. I'm going to hop in the shower and get out of these clothes so I can get more things organized and put up." She was happy to have a new place to live that was a little bigger than the last one. Although she wanted a big nice house now, she knew that she would have one eventually.

Around 10:00, Steve was getting in the shower then planning to lay down. Angelia was folding things up, and putting stuff away in the dresser drawers. She was wearing some little white see through shorts that hugged her ass with a sleeveless belly shirt. Her body was so sexy and perfect. Every time Steve looked at her, he wanted to make love to her.

"We gotta get some TV's. I'll try to grab one tomorrow," Steve said, laying back on the bed.

"Yeah, I figured I'll let you get the TV. You might want a certain kind."

"Not really. It don't matter to me. I'll take whatever one is on sale," he said, laughing. He lit a blunt of Kush that James had given him earlier, and puffed it a few times while he got comfortable. "You tryna hit this?"

She turned around and looked at him. "Not the blunt, but that right there." She smiled, pointing at his dick.

"Well you better come now before I go to sleep."

She set what was in her hands down and walked right over to the bed. She then pulled his dick out of his shorts and started sucking it while he was puffing his blunt. She started taking her shorts off at the same time. She soon climbed on top of his dick and inserted it inside her and started riding him until she made herself cum. He put his blunt down and turned her to the side as her ass poked out. First he licked and sucked her pussy, then he laid in back of her and slid his dick in and started stroking her wet pussy slowly.

"Yes, yes, Papi!" she moaned with one hand on his thigh, pulling him inside her. Her pussy was gushing juices out, and became wetter and wetter with every stroke. "Yes, Papi! That feels so good. Don't stop!" she moaned as her eyes rolled into the back of her head. As she felt his dick getting harder, she started moving her hips to his rhythm and soon felt his warm cum shoot inside her.

"Arggh! Shittt! This pussy . . . shit! This pussy so good, baby," he said as he squeezed his dick to the last drop inside her. She soon felt it leaking out of her, so she got up and went to the bathroom and sat on the toilet as she pushed it out. She then brought him a warm towel back to clean himself up.

"Let me finish putting these clothes up, and I'll come lay with you if you don't fall asleep."

He laughed. "If I do, just wake me up."

CHAPTER
FORTY-TWO

The next morning, Steve woke up to some good, gentle head from Angelia. He must have been in a deep sleep when she first started, because seconds after opening his eyes, he was cumming in her mouth, and she swallowed it all.

"Damn," he said as she laid down next to him. He then heard his phone start ringing. It was Juice.

"What's up, my dude?" he answered, tucking his dick back into his shorts.

"What's up, bro? You get right again yet? My phone going crazy."

Steve laughed. "Damn, already? No, I haven't. It's going to be a minute, but I will make sure I hit you up as soon as I'm ready."

"Bro, you have no idea. You ain't seen nothing yet." Juice started laughing. "I'm like Jordan out here, I'm telling you."

They both laughed.

"I see, I see."

"Let me know, bro. I am waiting on you."

"Okay, I'll holla at you as soon as I can. I'ma get on it," he said, getting up.

"Alright. Get at me."

Steve had to go see his uncle as soon as possible, so he got up and freshened up a little. He picked out some clothes and walked into the bathroom. Angelia came in behind him while he was brushing his teeth. She was wearing a big t-shirt with nothing underneath, and her nipples were poking right through.

"Where you going?" Angelia asked, folding her arms as she leaned her back against the door.

"To see my Uncle Swift. I got some stuff to talk about with him. I'll be back a little later today."

Angelia unfolded her arms and stood up straight. "Okay, I may be gone when you get back though. Me and Esha might go get something to eat."

Steve was quiet for a while. Angelia looked at him, almost as if she was seeking his permission or some type of reaction since she mentioned Esha's name. He finished rinsing his mouth, and Angelia proceeded to leave. Steve finally spoke up and replied to her.

"Alright. Hit me if you need me."

Angelia nodded and walked out of the bathroom. Steve phone alerted him and he pulled it out quickly. Looking down at his phone, he couldn't help but smile to himself. James had sent him a text telling him that it was done. Steve quickly called out to Angelia.

"Angelia! Aye! Angelia!" She came back looking a little bit worried. "Check that mail real quick for me please, boo," he told her.

"Oh, okay," she said as she put on her slippers and went downstairs, glad he wasn't tripping about her and Esha. She finally got downstairs and opened the front door, and what she saw had her a bit confused. She nodded her head before shouting out for Steve to come downstairs. "It's a car out here with a big red bow in the front yard," she said, still somewhat confused. "A really nice car too!"

Even from where she was standing, she could hear Steve laughing upstairs. She started wondering what he thought was so funny. Either way, he seemed pretty excited about it. She heard him coming down the stairs, and turned around to see him with a big grin on his face.

"That's yours boo!"

Angelia didn't know what to say. She looked at Steve, then looked back outside at the car, then back at Steve again, almost in disbelief. As the eye contact between her and Steve went on, she started to see that this wasn't some kind of joke.

"Steve, don't play with me." Steve shook his head with a big smile still plastered across his face. The feeling of pure joy and happiness was starting to overwhelm Angelia. She couldn't believe it. "Steve, please tell me that you not playing with me right now," she said, with the pitch of her voice getting higher and higher with each word. Steve shook his head again.

"I'm not playing with you, baby."

She stared at Steve for a moment longer in shock. Steve could see the light within her eyes intensify. He was overwhelmed with a feeling of satisfaction as he saw how happy he had made her. He beamed a wide smile at her again, and Angelia started jumping up and down, oozing with excitement.

"Shut up! Shut up! Oh, my God! Stop! Steve, don't play!" She then let out a loud scream and ran outside to check out the car. She ran around the car in circles a few times yelling then practically gave the car a hug. He got her a Cadillac ATS. It was a couple years old, but the new model, and it had low mileage. He had James drop it off to surprise her.

"Oh, my God! Oh, my God! Oh, my God!" she repeated again and again as she circled the car in excitement. She paused and looked at Steve, who was standing on the front porch smiling. The car was all black with black leather seats, and it was clean as a whistle. She ran her fingers and palms around on the car, touching it all over. She loved the way the car felt. It looked brand new. She kissed the car and hugged it again before turning around and looking back at Steve again, who was still enjoying watching her drool over the car.

"It's so nice!" she said with her hand over her mouth, still filled with surprise. She peeked into the window to check out the steering wheel, seats, and all the accessories. "I really have leather seats. Oh, my God!" she yelled out. She turned around to find Steve leaning calmly against the frame of the front door, with the keys to her car dangling in his right hand. Angelia ran to him, hugging him as tightly as she could while jumping up and down.

"I still can't believe you got me this! I love you so much!" she said as she jumped up on him, forgetting that his leg was still healing. He fell straight backwards, flat on the floor with her on top of him. She was completely oblivious to the pain she might have caused him, and was kissing him all over his face repeatedly. It was only after she stopped to look at him that she saw him gritting his teeth a little to endure the strain on his leg.

"Oh, shit! I'm sorry!" she said as she climbed off him. "I'm so sorry. I forgot you were still healing. Thank you, Papi! Thank you so much! I love you!"

He kept laughing as she went crazy, kissing him all over. "You welcome, baby."

CHAPTER
FORTY-THREE

Angelia stood back up and looked at the car, smiled, ran back outside with the keys, and got in to start it up. Steve watched her do a little celebration dance in the front seat. He stood there watching her for a few more seconds before going back upstairs to finish straightening himself up. While he finished getting ready, the image of Angelia's eyes and face lighting up at the sight of the car just couldn't leave his head. It was one of the most fulfilling things he had seen or felt. He felt so happy with himself, and he thought about how it would make him feel to see his mom walk into her new place. He loved doing things for others much more than doing things for himself.

When he came back downstairs, he glanced out the front door to find Angelia still in the car, making giggly sounds and messing with the buttons on the dashboard. He smiled as he got in his car.

"You gotta let me out, boo."

Angelia couldn't seem to talk to him anymore without smiling first. "Okay," she said, starting up the car.

As he drove away, Angelia was standing outside her car, smiling and waving at him. He couldn't stop thinking about her as he drove on, and he couldn't wipe the smile off his own face. He drove straight to see his uncle, getting on the freeway to get to Milan. The traffic was fairly light, although there was an accident right off the exit before the prison which slowed him down by about 10 minutes.

When Swift came through the door, he had a big smile on his face as usual. "Nephew! What's up, baby boy?"

"Nothing much, Unk." They hugged and sat down. Steve scooted his chair a little closer to Swift.

"So, how did everything turn out?"

Steve smiled to himself, then looked up at his uncle with big, bright eyes. Before he spoke, Swift knew everything he needed to know. He responded to Steve's smile with an even bigger one of his own. "Amazing. Absolutely amazing. You got more?"

Swift laughed. He already knew that he had the good shit, and he was glad that his nephew had made good with what he had given him to start with. He looked at Steve's face again. He could see a spark of determination in his eyes. They were the eyes of someone who wanted more, someone who was willing to work for it too. Steve was the type of young man that was ready to take all of the steps necessary to move all the way up, and that is exactly the kind of attitude that Swift liked to see, especially in his nephew, who he had been trying to wake up for a while now. He nodded to himself. He felt like Steve was ready for the next level. It was time for something bigger, something better, and perhaps something even more challenging.

"Alright, nephew. You did good. I'm going to link you up with this lady in Texas," he said, writing down her name and address for him. "This is her restaurant. She cooks there. Go up there and ask for her. Her name is Karo, pronounced Catho, the R is silent. She won't get mad if you pronounce it wrong. She's used to it. But tell her you're Swift from Michigan's nephew and you want to work." Steve nodded, trying to pay close attention to every word Swift was saying.

Swift continued, "Tell her that I sent you. Now, if she starts feeling on you, let her. She may be feeling for a wire. And don't take your phone in there. She is going to ask you where you want them delivered. Tell her where, and don't make it where you lay your head at neither. Then she will give you a price. That shit up and down, so I can't say what it will be, but it will be sweet. The quality of what she is going to have is not going to be what you just had. Those came from elsewhere. But with hers, you can take four and a half ounces out and add the cut I gave you if you have more left. If not, hit the dude I told you about last time and tell him you are there for Swift's favor. He will give you 5,000 grams of cut. It's already paid for."

Steve nodded again before he said, "Okay, I got it. What do you want for each kilo I move?"

"$1,000 even, but I want $5,000 for the cut. That shit a thousand a key."

"It's worth it though, Unk."

"Shit, trust me, I know. That's how I made my first million."

"Damn, so is it cheaper if I get them from Texas myself?"

"Yeah, it is, but if you want them guaranteed, just let them go ahead and do what they do."

"How much cheaper would it be though?"

"Bout $3,000 per kilo, sometimes more"

"Damn," Steve said as his mind started wandering like crazy.

"So you got rid of everything already?"

"I ain't got even a crumb left, Unk. I'm mad as hell."

Swift laughed. "Damn, that was fast as fuck."

"Man, they loved it too. And one person got all that. I haven't had a chance to reach out to nobody else yet."

CHAPTER
FORTY-FOUR

Swift seemed surprised, and relatively impressed, at the same time. "You got one person that took all that in just a few days?"

"Yeah, he woulda took more too if I had it."

At first, Steve had thought that maybe Swift didn't think it was a good idea that one person took everything, but seeing his uncle's reaction, he started to think that he had done things right after all. He figured that the less people involved, the less opportunity there was for a mistake, and his uncle seemed to agree.

"I would stick to just him if I was you. You don't really need no one else, unless you just trying to turn up."

Steve smiled. "I'm trying to turn up, Unk. I ain't gone play with you."

"Well, you a grown man. You do what you do, nephew. You just make sure you are being smart out there, staying off that phone, not being greedy, and of course, stacking your money."

Suddenly, Swift's face changed significantly and the laughter in his voice was gone. He was now being very real with Steve.

"Niggas don't get these types of opportunities often. They trusted me for years, and I never was late paying. I never told, and I always did what I was supposed to do, so you have to be the same way. Don't front shit out if you can't afford to pay for it. This lady may give you more than you can handle. You're going to be getting cars loaded, with the title, and a lot of other free shit. It will all be a gift from her though. So, I'm just trying to give you a heads up. Don't play with these people. Matter of fact, don't even think about playing with them. Them mutherfuckers dangerous. This that real TV type shit. I know you wouldn't, but I have to say it. I trust that you'll be smart with everything. If I didn't, we wouldn't be having this conversation."

"You don't have to worry about that, Unk. Ever."

"My nigga," Swift said. He hugged him and kissed his forehead. He felt very safe and confident that Steve would do the right thing. "You was raised well, so I know you know to take care of your people, close ones, and family always."

"Yeah, for sure. I'm on it, Unk."

"Good. You can deposit the $5,000 in this account again. And call Sabrina when you get at least $100,000 to give her."

"Got it." Steve was taking notes on some of the things his uncle was telling him.

"Make sure you are investing into businesses too. Don't be fucking around buying liabilities, you hear me?"

"Yeah, I know, Unk."

"What's the difference between an asset and a liability?"

"An asset puts money in your pocket, and a liability takes money out."

"Fucking right," Swift replied, nodding again. Steve had been saying all the right things since he walked through the door, and Swift was happy to hear all of it. "That's good, nephew. You seem like you learning the right things. I see you started that book I told you to get."

"Yes, I started it. I'm not too deep into it though, yet."

"Well get deep ASAP. Name five assets."

"Dump truck, semi-truck, box truck. Damn, I'm naming all trucks out here. Hold on. A house can be an asset if you're not living in it and it's bringing you money in, but it's not one if you are living in it, and it's taking money out of your pockets."

Swift raised an eyebrow.

"Hold on. Say that last one again."

"A house is an asset if you are not living in it, but renting it out or AirBnB'ing it out makes it an asset."

"Exactly. Okay, name some liabilities."

"Cars, clothes, watches, jewelry, and entertainment."

"Good. Good. Assets can be vending machines, salons, restaurants, etc. Just as long as it's paying you, it's an asset."

"Got it, Unk. You know I appreciate you and all you doing for me. This shit is literally changing my life."

"It's all love, nephew," Swift replied. He leaned in towards Steve and nudged him playfully on his left shoulder and whispered, "So, did you get you, or should I say us, some pussy?"

Steve couldn't help but start smiling. Shila instantly came into his mind. "Yeah, Unk. I told you I was going to."

CHAPTER
FORTY-FIVE

They started laughing, and Swift couldn't help but clap for Steve a little. That's exactly what he wanted to hear. "Is she a baddie?"

"She actually is. She got her own shit. A nice ass house, a Benz truck, and she owns a company that runs dump trucks and shit."

"Damn, for real? Where you meet her at?"

"I used to go to school with her. She said she been had a crush on me, but I was with someone at the time."

"Oh, yeah? Man, you got to keep that one. Those ones are hard to find, and she doing all that. That's what you call an asset type of woman. She can actually show you how to make money with the trucking, and she can for sure teach you other things. I ain't saying marry her, I'm just saying, iron sharpens iron, so two people that's grinding together is better than one. I don't know her, but keep dicking her down."

Steve put his hand on his head, scratching and rubbing it nervously. Since his uncle was in his presence and he needed advice, he decided to bring up the topic he had been wanting to discuss.

"Man, I don't know. Me and my girl been working things out. I don't think I wanna keep cheating."

Swift now seemed unimpressed for the first time since Steve had arrived. He shook his head in sadness. "Listen to me, nephew. I don't care what you and that girl you caught in your bed with another man is working out. This new girl you got, keep her around and keep fucking her. I'm telling you. I know you love your little girlfriend, but she fucked up. No doubt about it. I'm not going to go deep into all of the details right now, because you may not understand it fully right now, or you might not be fully ready to believe it. But, like I told you before, when a person show you who they are, believe them."

Although Steve understood where Swift was coming from, he was really looking for a way to either handle both of them in a way that was convenient for him, or how to let one of them go as peacefully as possible, particularly Shila. After nervously shuffling his feet around for a second, he looked up at Swift and replied, "I think me and Angelia can make it work though, Unk."

Swift paused and looked at him for a few seconds before replying. "Try it out. Me personally . . . I'm not the kind of man that can accept a woman back after something like that. Maybe I'm right, or maybe I'm wrong, who knows? It may or may not work for you, nephew. I can't tell your heart what to do. I can only tell you what I'd do in your situation, and I think I been pretty clear about where I stand on that."

"What if I don't want to have sex with the other girl anymore, and I just want to be friends so she could help me with new shit?"

Swift thought for a moment, then looked at his nephew and took a deep breath. "Was the sex and head good?"

"A1, amazing," Steve said, turning red.

Swift shook his head hard after hearing that comment. "I think you wouldn't be able to resist her if you keep hanging around her. She obviously likes you, so she gonna try to make her moves, and eventually you gone break. If you stop fucking her, she would likely eventually just cut you off. You already cheated and fucked her, so I'd just keep it up," Swift said, shrugging at first, then laughing while giving Steve a wink. "I'm kidding, nephew. Do what your heart tell you to. If you want to be a faithful man to that girlfriend of yours, be that. There is nothing wrong with that. I'd like to see you spend that energy on someone that was faithful back to you, but that's your choice. One thing I do know is that if Karo find you attractive, you better knock the dust off that pussy."

They both laughed.

"Deal," Steve said, slapping his hand.

"So, how old is the girl that you fucking on the side? Do she have any kids?"

"27 or 28 . . . my age. She has two kids and two baby daddies."

"I'll be the third for sure," he joked. "Boy, you just don't know what you got. Is she bossy like trying to boss you around, because you know sometimes them independent women be thinking they wear the pants and shit."

"Naw, I don't get that from her. She knows her shit, but I think she more the girly, submissive type. She wants to help me and teach me some things, but it ain't like she tryna tell me what to do or anything. On the other hand, she is aggressive and dominant in the bedroom, but I like that," Steve said, laughing.

Swift couldn't stop nodding his head in approval. "Oh, now that's cool. Damn, dawg, she seems impressive. Everything you been saying about her sounds good to me. Okay, so how old is your main lady?"

"27, no kids."

The condescending tone in Swift's voice that always showed up when he spoke about Angelia returned, and Steve picked up on it right away. "What she got going on? What can you say about her?"

Steve laughed. "Man, don't do that. She got potential. She getting herself together."

Swift nodded, but he wasn't having any of it. He just wished he could somehow show Steve that messing around with Angelia for much longer was going to be nothing but trouble for him in the long run. He knew Steve was deeply in love with her, but he also wanted Steve to understand that sometimes a man has to make difficult choices. He wanted him to know that the choices that are the most difficult to make are often exactly what's needed to achieve great things in life. To him, Shila sounded like a woman that knew what she wanted, where she was coming from, and where she wanted to go. He was even more impressed that she had two children and was still able to have her life and money at the level she did at such a young age. He strongly believed that Shila was the type of woman that would be a significant benefit to Steve's life at the stage he was currently in. But he also knew Steve wouldn't be able to take his advice to heart until something even worse happened. He didn't want to stress Steve out about it too much, but he had made up his mind about Angelia. He was pretty sure everything was going to play out eventually. He just hoped it wouldn't be too late for Steve by the time he realized what he was dealing with.

CHAPTER
FORTY-SIX

"If it looks like a duck, and quacks like a duck, it's a duck, nephew. I don't know what else to tell you, but you need to think about trusting me on this one. But I know you ain't gone listen to me. You still going off looks. You still young so I'ma just drop the subject. I'ma leave you alone about it."

"Thank you," Steve replied, and then they both started laughing. "Oh, yeah. The side girl, well, her name Shila. She also was talking to me about the stock market and crypto currency."

That was it. Swift could barely hide his displeasure at this point. This was a woman who knew all the right shit to do, and Steve still wanted to be with a cheater because of her looks. He wanted Steve to stop talking.

"See, man, don't tell me nothing else about that girl unless you den knocked her up or about to marry her. You don't even know what to do with that right there. You might as well let me have that one when I come home, since you don't have a damn clue," he joked and laughed.

"We supposed to meet today though to talk about the dump truck business. She gone show me some trucks and talk to me about the different kinds and all that."

"Make sure you give her what she wants too."

They laughed. Steve shook his head, then leaned back in his chair.

"I'll think about, Unk. I'm trying to be good."

"You going to need her for way more than that. You have to look at the big picture, trust me. Little angry Angelia going to be okay. Keep doing your thing until she step her game up, because as of right now, she ain't on nothing. What if you have to do time one day? God forbid. How Angelia gone feed you in here if she ain't got nothing? And you think she gone stay loyal while you in here if she ain't stayed loyal while you out there with her? You're making a big mistake, but I've said enough."

"I'll figure out how to eat, just as long as she writes me and comes to see me."

Swift almost slid out of the chair he was sitting on, collapsing to the floor. He couldn't believe what he was hearing. His nephew might be even more far gone than he thought. After recomposing himself, he said, "Damn, nephew. You got the game all twisted. See, me . . . can't no broke girls even be in my life. Not for a short time, not for a long time. I just ain't got time for someone like that. It's a requirement for my women to have a 700 or better credit score, their own house, car, job and a business on the side or we can't even date!"

Steve laughed. "Damn, Unk. You really be doing it like that, huh?"

"Hell yeah! I'm that way now because I had to learn the hard way by doing shit the way you doing it right now. Chasing looks, big booties, and shit. You ain't going nowhere with all that shit. One thing is for sure, looks fade. And after they do, what you got left? Ask yourself that. That new girl you fucking right there, she know how the world work. She finna show you the ropes if you put in the work, but you still hung up on Angelia pretty ass. You ever get in a situation where you out of sight, you will see exactly what I'm talking about. I'm telling you now, it will be better for you to ditch the bitch," Swift finished with a chuckle.

"You killing me, Unk!"

Swift laughed. "Okay, okay. I quit, Mr. Hamburger."

"Aw, so I'ma ham now? What you saying?"

"I mean, you doing what hams do."

They both started laughing again and continued talking for a couple more hours. Steve always enjoyed talking with his uncle. He knew Swift always gave the best advice, whether or not it was the easy path to take. His uncle always had something new to help him with whenever Steve was in some kind of pickle. He loved Swift's company, and even though their conversations would go on for hours, Steve would be so immersed in all the talking that he would loose track of time. Swift would too, but more than anything, he loved passing on knowledge to the next generation.

Swift was glad to be around his nephew every now and then, keeping him company, and helping him out with all his issues, especially when it came to money. He just wished Steve would take his advice on the whole Shila and Angelia thing. Swift knew that even if a man was successful and got his money up, all that shit could be ruined, including the man himself, if he didn't have the right woman by his side, supporting him and having his back. There was nothing that Steve could say to rationalize or justify staying with Angelia to Swift that would make any sense.

No matter what, Angelia was not that woman. He didn't even know her, and he already had all the evidence he needed.

If Steve wasn't going to see the big black cloud that Angelia had over her, Swift was hoping that he would at least see the bright ray of sunshine that Shila would be in his life. Even though he tried to be empathetic with Steve's situation, Swift couldn't help but bring the conversation back to Shila over and over again. Steve brushed it off though as 'Unk was just being Unk' and would try to change the topic to something else. Over the course of the conversation, Swift stopped stressing it though, and knew that Steve had made up his mind to learn the hard way, and that he would understand what was going on once everything started to play out.

CHAPTER
FORTY-SEVEN

After hours of talking, Steve was finally up and out of there, back on a mission to get back to the money. Despite what he felt to be some negativity toward Angelia coming from Swift, all in all, Steve was pumped and motivated to go hard based on their conversation. He was focused and determined, and nothing, absolutely nothing, was going to stop him. When he sat down in his car, he checked his phone to find messages or missed calls from Shila, Angelia, James, and his mom.

Shila: Hey, boo. Just making sure we still on for today.

Steve: Yes we are. I will text you shortly. Just got done visiting my uncle. We maybe can do it earlier.

Shila: Okay. That sounds great. Just let me know!

He then opened up Angelia's text and she had written him something a little lengthy. She was telling him how much she loved him and wanted to be with him and how they have come so far. She also let him know that she could see that he was stepping up his game and she was proud of him. He sent a few messages, addressing what he felt were the major points in her long message, but didn't have the desire to write paragraphs back to her. He closed her message and opened up the next one, which was from his mom. His mom told him that she was ready when he was, and that she had found the perfect duplex. Steve decided that it was the next most important conversation he needed to have, and he didn't want to text, so he called her.

"Hey, son!" she answered.

"Hey, mom. So you found a nice one?"

"Yes, I'm going to send you a picture. It's not really a trailer. They call these modular homes. It's pretty much the same thing because you can move it wherever you want, but it looks just like a house, baby. This one is so nice. It has 3 bedrooms, 3 bathrooms, the works, baby. They only want $50,000 for it. I told them I had $15,000 to put down and they said I can move in right now if I give them that. So I am ready when you are." She giggled a little then said, "I'm all packed up and ready to go."

Steve loved hearing the excitement in his mother's voice. He couldn't wait to see the look on her face when she walked into her new place. "Okay, sounds good. Send me a picture so I can check it out. Do you need new furniture?"

"Well, I have a sofa, and a table, but -."

"Don't worry about taking that stuff. I'll have Angelia take you furniture shopping probably later on today. Let me see what's up."

"So today we are moving?"

"Yeah, today, momma."

"Yayyy!" she screamed in excitement. "Okay, baby. Call me when you're ready. I'll be here!"

"Okay, momma. Call you in second." He clicked over as he saw James calling.

"What's up, bro?" he answered.

"Juice keeps calling me. What you done did to that nigga? He den fell in love with yo' ass."

Steve laughed.

James continued saying, "For real, he said he waiting on you. I was just calling to tell you that. He scared me at first. I thought something happened, but that nigga was on the phone so damn happy."

"Yeah, we been good. I definitely appreciate his ass."

"The feeling is mutual then. What you up to?"

"Just leaving prison, hollering at Unk."

"Oh, okay. What Angelia say when she seen the car?"

"Man, she went crazy. She was running circles around that bitch, screaming and shit. She ran at me and knocked my ass down and shit telling me thank you, thank you, kissing me and everything. Good looking, bro."

"No problem. You know I got you, fasho. How that leg doing?"

"Shit, a nigga walking normal. I be forgetting about it. It did kinda go out though when she jumped on me, but as far as walking, I'm walking normal. I ain't got no pain or nothing. My uncle didn't notice. He ain't say shit."

"Oh, that's good to hear."

"What you got up?"

"Man, I been working in the basement, you already know. Shit is coming together."

"Fasho, can't wait to get that going."

"I'm on it. It won't be long, that's fasho. I just cloned all kinda shit, so really we rocking and rolling now."

"That's what's up."

"Oh, I grabbed them two things for you too. You going to love them."

"Oh, good. I need those. I should be at the crib in like an hour if you want to meet me there."

"Yeah, that works. I'll see you in a lil' bit, bro."

James had got Steve the two guns that he asked for. They were two black .40 caliber pistols with extended clips on both of them.

CHAPTER
FORTY-EIGHT

Steve drove home thinking about the trip to Texas, and thought about when would be the best time for him to leave. He didn't really want to leave before Angelia left to go to Cali. He looked at the time, and it was still early, so he decided to meet with James to get his guns first. When he got to James' house, he came in the door, and James had them both sitting on the table.

"Damn, these nice," Steve said, picking both of them up and examining them. He nodded his head approvingly as he set them back down.

"Hell yeah," James replied. "You lucky I didn't keep them for myself. I'ma have to get me some of them for myself, but I think I might roll with a 9mm. I don't need no extended clip though. They just opened up that new gun range off the freeway last week, and I might go up there and check a few guns out. They got ones you can rent, so I'ma try a few out and see what I like. They be having tactical pistol competitions and all kinds of shit if someone really wanna get into that shit."

"Hell yeah, I heard about that new range. I ain't interested in no tactical competitions or anything like that, but shit, I'll go up there and shoot with you sometime."

James nodded, and slapped his hand.

"Shit, bro. My mom found a new crib. I'm about to go check it out and get her settled in. I called a moving truck so she ain't gotta do much, but I wanna be there when she sees it for the first time. She's gonna leave most of her furniture, so I'ma have Ang take her furniture shopping."

"Man, that's good news. Shit, hit me later then, bro."

Moments later, Steve was out the door. When he got to his mom's house, the moving company was there, already packing things into their truck. They were done in under an hour, since most of the large items were staying behind. Steve followed his mom and the moving truck to the new place, and stayed while they unloaded everything. His mom looked like she was in a dream, how she was walking around, describing to him what she wanted to do and where. He was so happy to see her excited about her new home.

Within no time, the moving company was done, and Steve signed the paperwork, and they left. He called Angelia to see what she was doing and see if she wanted to go furniture shopping with his mom, but she was busy, so he took her up to the store himself. They picked out everything she needed, including a TV for her living room, and a TV for her bedroom. Luckily, they could deliver everything the following day, so his mom wouldn't have to go long without it.

Steve followed her back to her place, and made sure she got in okay. He asked if she needed anything else, but she said she was fine for now. As he looked around, he was pleased with the place his mom picked out. It looked exactly like a house. You couldn't tell that it had been pre-built in a factory at all.

Steve had a lot to do, so he had to get going. His mom was so happy that she didn't want him to leave, but she understood. He promised that he would be back to visit her soon, and make sure the furniture was what she wanted after it was all in place.

When he left, he was feeling like he should really go ahead and take his trip to Texas even before Angelia left on hers. He didn't want to waste any time. He knew that Juice was already waiting, so the sooner he made the trip, the sooner he could put him back on. He had to keep focused, and make the right moves without letting any distractions delay him.

It was about 5 p.m. by the time he got on the freeway, and he called up Shila to confirm that she was still able to meet. She told him that she was ready when he was, so he drove up to the trucking yard where she kept her trucks. When he pulled in, he saw that the place was packed with all different kinds of semi-trucks and trailers. It was like a whole new world he had never seen or heard about before. Guys were working on their trucks, washing them, parking them, and more. It was exciting to him as he drove through the yard, and he got even more excited when he saw Shila waving him over. He pulled up next to her truck and parked. Shila was looking gorgeous even in her simple leggings, fitted t-shirt, and sneakers. Her body was sexy, and she was curvy in all the right places. She beamed a big, beautiful smile at him when she saw him parking and stepping out of the car.

CHAPTER
FORTY-NINE

"Hey, boo!" she exclaimed as she ran towards him with her arms open. As she approached, Steve couldn't take his eyes off her chest, bouncing as she ran. After seeing that sight, he couldn't resist her. He stretched his arms open to receive her in all her excitement. As she leaped on him, Steve staggered backwards.

She kissed him on the lips and hugged him tightly. "It's been forever! Let me find out you're running from me!"

He laughed as she slowly released him from her embrace. "Chill out. Ain't nobody running from you. I'm right here, sexy."

"Okay, good. Because I'll come and find you if I have to," she joked.

"You silly," he replied. He then stopped to look around. "Which ones are yours?"

"These two right here," she said proudly. "They twins." She walked towards the two trucks parked a few feet away from Steve then she gave one a pat on the hood. "They dirty right now though. Dump trucks are hard to keep clean, so don't even try."

Steve could tell she was excited to show them off to him.

"Damn, you got the big shit," he said as he walked around them, checking them out. She had two Mack trucks that were a medium blue and grey. "So are there different sizes or what?"

"Yep. These two are called quads. A quad stands for 4 axles. You see these tires back here?" she asked as she pointed at the tires on one of the trucks. "1, 2, 3, 4. Now, you could do a tri-axle, which is 3 tires here in the back. I wouldn't go any smaller than that. You could also do a Cinco, which is 5 tires running on the side. A Cinco is the big boy right after this one, but I think the quads are prefect. They've always worked out good for me. They are not too small and not too big."

"Oh, okay, okay. Is this manual or automatic?"

"All my trucks are manuals. I thought about getting an automatic, but my dad would turn over in his grave if I did that. I can hear him yelling at me right now. He was not for automatic nothing," she said with a smile.

He laughed. "Why not?"

"He just said a manual is way better on gas, and gives you a lot more control to get out of messy situations. Like if you stuck in the mud or going up a steep hill, a manual is better. That's what he would always say. I like them though and I have no complaints."

"Okay. That's good to know. So how much do one of these cost?"

"Well, these are $100,000 a piece, and I bought them used."

"Damn!"

She giggled. "Hold on, wait. We got them basically new. I'm a woman, so I'm not going to buy a super used truck. I don't have time to be going back and forth to shops getting stuff fixed. I'd rather spend that time with my kids, or with you," she said, giving him a wink. "I'm not saying a new truck can't break down, because they can and they have. But my daddy always told me to get good trucks, and good equipment. But there are guys out there getting money that have paid $20,000, $30,000, $40,000, or $50,000 for their trucks and they have the potential to make the same money as I do, or even more. It all depends on what works for you, and how you wanna do it."

"Oh, so the companies you get these jobs through don't care about the year of your truck?"

"Well, the company I'm with does. For the company I'm with now, your truck can't be more than 6 years old, but some companies don't care at all. As long as you get the work done or make the delivery, they good."

"So your trucks are paid off or you letting them pay for themselves?"

"Everything is paid for."

"Damn, that's what's up. And how much one truck make a day?"

"Mines make about $850 gross. I spend about $50 in gas a day maybe, because the contract I have is just a 15 mile radius back and forth all day, well 10 hours. I pay my driver $20 an hour, and I pocket the $600, Monday through Saturday. And also, some jobs run two shifts, so that $600 can be doubled daily, just a side note. And remember that's just for one of the trucks."

CHAPTER
FIFTY

"Т hat's sweet. So what kind of license do the drivers need and where do you find them?"

"They need to have a CDL B with at least a year of experience to work for me. This is a real simple job, and anybody can do it. I did it before. All you doing is pulling up, getting on the little CB radio in there, and telling them how much to put in the box. They load you and you go and dump it at a place down the street, then go back and do it again. With this job, you don't even need the CB radio. It's the same thing every day, so all you doing is pulling up, and they already know what's up."

"Dang, that sounds cool. Where can I get a CDL B? What do it cost?"

"It's cheap, under $100, I think. You just taking a test at the Secretary of State. A CDL B is basically a chauffer's license, for like buses, box trucks. It's easy to get though. A CDL A is for the big semi-trucks and stuff with the long trailers," she said, pointing at a few trucks around the yard.

"Ohhhh, okay, okay. So is a dump truck hard to drive?"

"Not at all. It's basically like driving a big U-Haul truck. It's easy."

"So, can I finance one of these or do I gotta pay cash up front?"

"Yeah, you can. What's your credit like? I have a commercial equipment bank that would give anyone with a 600 credit score or higher a loan with 15% down."

"That's not bad."

"No, not bad at all, especially with the money you'll be making. A commercial equipment lender is who you'll want to go through for sure. It's easier and better than going through a normal bank or credit union. A lot of banks and credit unions don't mess with commercial loans or equipment because to them, it's risky I guess. A lot of people try to get commercial loans through their banks or credit unions and get denied, even with a 700 credit score. Plus they been banking there for years, and they're still getting turned down. Or they might do something like ask you for a business plan, business taxes and all kinds of other documents that make the process much more difficult. But if you got a commercial equipment lender, which you can find thousands of just on Google, you will have way better luck getting the loan for your truck or trailer. And it will be much less of a headache too."

"That's deep. I never even heard of a commercial lender."

"A lot of people haven't, but now you know just in case you ever need it."

"You turning me on with all this information," he told her.

"Well, let me keep it coming then. I have more and more for you," she replied, smiling.

He laughed. "Okay, so what is the first things I need to do if I want to start my own trucking company, hauling state to state and stuff."

"Well, think of a name and a logo."

"Naw, I got all that. I'm talking like LLC, then that DOT number, and all the stuff you got on the side of your truck? How do I go about getting all that?"

"I think it was about $500 for my LLC the way I did it, but you can do it for yourself way cheaper, but I didn't know at first. I would have done it for $50," she said, laughing. "So set up the LLC, and open a bank account once you got all your LLC paperwork in. You going to be hauling state to state?"

"Yeah."

"So you will have to get your own authority, which is a MC number. That's your motor carrier number, which will allow you to take stuff from state to state. You may have to write all this down. You want me to make you a checklist later?"

He laughed. "Yeah, you right."

"Because you have to get a DOT number, MC number, an Apportion plate, these fuel stickers called IFTA, and then you have to sign up for load boards. So, yeah. I'll make you a list, boo."

"Okay, okay. How the load boards work?"

"It's simple. You just sign up. It may cost for a good one. Like dat.com, I think is around $60 a month. You just go on there, for example, let's say you're coming from Michigan and you want to go to, say Kentucky. You just put in both states or add cities to narrow your search, then all the loads they have for today will pop up. If you see something good like $2,000 for something that weighs 25,000 pounds, one pick up and one drop off, that might be something you want to take."

"Oh, okay. I see. So who these loads come from?"

"On Dat.com, it's a lot of brokers and companies, so basically it's a pool of companies posting all their loads for independent trucking companies to grab. If you like the company you haul for, you can easily be like, y'all have these loads every day? If so, I want all of them. I would only do something like that if I had something coming back from Kentucky every day too, because if the company only got loads every day from Michigan to Kentucky, but nothing coming back, you gotta figure it out or drive back empty."

"Damn, okay. What you doing sounds a lot easier. What if I gave you $100,000 to get a truck, could you put the truck under your company and we do some kind of split or something?"

She smiled. "If you was mine, yeah, but I'll think about it and see if we might be able to make something work. Just be my boyfriend so we can just run it up," she said, giggling.

He laughed. "See there you go."

They both laughed.

"I'm not about to boss a nigga up for the next bitch can have him."

"Damn, you gone make money too. I'm trying to cut you in."

She giggled. "Cut me in? No, I can just buy another truck, boo, and that's that. But I'll show you how to do this for free. You just gotta set your own company up."

"Naw, I want to be under yours."

"Well, that's going to come with some baby making, mister."

They both laughed.

CHAPTER
FIFTY-ONE

one and give me a baby, and you can add all the trucks you want. I'll manage everything, drivers and all, plus I got an 800 credit score and bringing 6 figures in yearly where it ain't shit for me to spend $100,000 and have to worry about the Feds or the IRS. Sooo, you let me know what you wanna do, boo boo," she said, joking as she snapped her fingers, knowing she had her shit together.

"See, you tryna blackmail me and shit."

"I'm not. I'll show you how to set up your own company if you willing to do the work."

She didn't believe he had that kind of money anyway. She just didn't want to insult him. Steve couldn't tell through her tone, though. She was being careful with everything she said.

"I understand that. Sounds like I gotta cuff you first."

"You can cuff me second. What is you saying?"

They both laughed at how silly she was. She was always making him laugh when she said certain things to him.

"You always be laughing at me like I be playing with your ass. Ain't nobody playing with you," she said, giggling.

He laughed and grabbed her from behind, roughly squeezing her. She relaxed her body in his grip, and already, they could feel the heat of the sexual tension between them. Swift was right; Steve was going to have a hard time resisting her. He leaned in and breathed on her neck and whispered, "I don't be thinking you're playing. You just so blunt, it be funny."

"I just go for what I want, that's all," Shila replied with a whisper of her own before turning around and kissing him with her soft, glossy lips. Steve received her kiss, and then planted an even gentler one on her lips in return. She pulled away from him to look him in the eyes once more. "Even with me talking about your raggedy Impala, I'm still trying to be with you. That should tell you something right there."

He laughed. "My car ain't raggedy," he finally said.

She giggled. "I'm just saying, I actually like you as a person, and I know you can do better. You just need a chick like me, that's all. I told you, let me upgrade you."

"I can upgrade at any time, boo. My car ain't got nothing to do with nothing. Rich people drive Impalas."

"You right, but notice what they're rich in, and then pay attention to if they are black, white, Asian, or whatever. You a black man from Pontiac, which means you may have to look like money to really attract others with money to help you and give you a shot. I'm not saying clothes and flashy jewelry and petty things like that. I'm just talking about a decent car. People tend to take you more seriously if you're driving something that's respectable.

Steve couldn't help but smile at Shila's words. "You sound like my uncle. He would say something like that. And I respect what he says, so that's saying something about you right there."

"See, you know I'm not just talking. If I wouldn't have known you from school, I would have never spoke to you driving that. So basically, you wouldn't even be able to talk to a chick in my league driving a car like that. It may sound messed up, but test it. Go to Farmington, West Bloomfield, or another city where the people got money and try to get a chick in traffic," she said, giggling. "She ain't even gone look your way. She gone be scared, thinking you gone rob her or something."

He laughed. "That's funny. That's some shallow ass shit, but you probably right."

"It is, but that's pretty much how society is, and you know that."

"So if we were together, would you have a problem with me driving this?"

"No, not at all, because we doing our thing. The proof is in the pudding. See, once you have money, you can do what you want, and can't nobody tell you shit. But before you do, you gotta prove yourself, and sometimes that means looking some type of way, just so you can get a chance with the right people."

"Ohh, I see what you saying. That actually makes sense. Who taught you all this stuff?"

She giggled. "My daddy mostly. He stayed in my ears. He was kind of like you. You wouldn't think he had money, but he owned all kinds of stuff. He drove a regular car and everything. He told me he never drove a flashy car because with all the knowledge he had, he didn't need anyone. He made it to where people needed him."

"Got it. He sounds like he was a pretty smart man."

"For sure."

"Okay, we gone have to figure something out soon. I'm starving, and I need to eat."

"I got something for you to eat right in the back seat," she joked.

CHAPTER
FIFTY-TWO

He smiled. "Come on. Climb in there and keep that ass tooted."

"Say no more." She opened the back door and crawled over the seats and left her ass up in the air.

"Oh, you serious," he said, licking his lips. He followed her into the back seat and slowly pulled her leggings down, revealing her pussy lips. He licked his fingers and started gently rubbing her lips between his fingers. He rubbed each of her lips individually, then rubbed right in the middle of them, without sticking his finger inside her. Shila already had her eyes closed and was waiting to sink into the pleasure.

"Let me see," he said as he pulled his fingers away from her pussy lips and replaced them with his tongue. He started off by licking between her lips a few times then spitting on it. He reintroduced his fingers into the mix, and stuck his index finger in while licking her clit. He licked and sucked to the sound of her moaning. He was getting the reaction he had hoped for.

"Damn, you eat this pussy so good!" she moaned.

He kept licking and sucking, spreading her ass cheeks until he heard her say, "Don't stop. Right there!" He kept going and going until she tensed up and came. Her body twitched, and her legs started to vibrate. The moans coming out of her mouth broke the silence, and she was then completely silent again as her body shook and the cream flowed out from between her lips and down her legs. He licked the cream from her legs, all the way back up to her pussy. Then, like a vacuum, he sucked all her juices up and it sent chills throughout her entire body.

"Oh, my God," she whispered trying to catch her breath. She was completely caught up in the moment. Apart from the way the orgasm felt in the first place, this was now the first time she was experiencing some sort of immediate post-orgasmic pleasure. It was exhilarating for her. She collapsed in her back seat and just looked at him while he stood outside her door wiping his mouth off. She started daydreaming, imagining them together and how she would dress him and show him how a man should be treated. She wanted Steve. She wanted all of him, not just sexually either. She wanted him to be hers and only hers, and most of all, she hoped that he would give her the opportunity to show him how much.

"You need to stop playing and just let me love you," she finally said as she regained her breath.

"Huh?"

"We need to just be together, but you playing."

"Chill out. I'm in a whole relationship. I ain't even supposed to be doing this, let alone what you over there talking about."

"Yeah, but you know she ain't shit, duh. But, okay. Whatever, I'll stop saying it." She pulled her leggings up. "You eat my pussy so good. I never came that fast off head, and that little thing you did, sucking them juices out of me, that was something else. I never felt like that before." She took a deep breath and got out of the back. "What am I gone do with you?"

He laughed. "That's how I be feeling when you put that pussy on me!"

"Oh it is? You about to be getting more of this then."

They both started laughing. Steve knew she was dead ass serious. From the way she looked at him, and the way her eyes danced around him, he could tell that she still wanted some more of him. He felt reluctant to take it further, because they were in a relatively public place. Shila, though, didn't care much about prying eyes. She wanted what she wanted, and she wanted it immediately.

"Get in," she said, smiling. Steve couldn't help but smirk.

"You trying to do it right here?"

"Ain't nobody paying attention to us. I got tints, come on."

He laughed. "You crazy."

He stared at her for a bit longer, looking deep into her eyes. He could see that she wasn't joking. After that, he nodded to himself and started getting in while she scooted the driver's seat forward. She got in and started pulling down his pants to pull out his dick. Even though it wasn't rock hard yet, she still liked the way it felt in her hands. She stroked it for a moment while looking at it, feeling it slowly grow in her hands. She wanted his dick all to herself. The longer she stared at it, the more she wanted it until she couldn't hold back anymore. She started sucking his dick until he was rock hard. He could tell by the way she was sucking, that she was trying her best to make him belong to her. As she sucked away, she suddenly slowed down because she didn't want him to cum in her mouth. Not yet. She wanted him inside her. Once his dick was standing at it's peak, twitching periodically as the blood in his erection throbbed, she took one leg out of her legging and sat on his dick, first inserting just the tip, then pausing before sitting all the way down and letting out a long, quiet moan. She loved the way it felt when it slid inside her slowly, stretching her out and filling her up. His dick felt so hard and warm, and she was rolling her eyes almost all the way to the back of her head just from the initial sensation.

She rocked back and forth on his dick, slowly at first, but steadily going faster and faster before saying, "Mmmmm, you gone have to cum in me. I'll take a Plan B."

He looked up at her, with a serious expression suddenly overtaking his face, and she burst out laughing. "I will. I will, I promise," she said, then started working his dick inside her, slowly. She moved her hips back and forth, and then around in a circle, using his shaft to stir up her insides. He could feel his dick getting more sensitive, and he was loving the sensation. She then started bouncing on it, slowly at first, then faster, and faster, until you could hear the sound of the impact of her thighs off of him. She started to moan loudly, and Steve was loving what she was doing with his dick. He loved watching the expression on her face, and listening to the sounds she made. He was getting more and more into it, just watching her do her thing. Then he grabbed her booty cheeks tightly, and took control for himself, bouncing her up and down even faster and harder on his dick. The clapping and smacking sounds grew louder and louder.

"Yes! Yes! Yes! Yes!" she screamed as he slammed her down on his dick again and again. She was loving him taking control of her body.

Her pussy felt so good to him. It was soft, wet, warm, and gripping his dick perfectly as she slid up and down. He could feel every section of her insides, and something about her pussy had him growing weak. He closed his eyes as he could feel the cum approaching. He concentrated the entirety of his mind on the sensations that his dick could feel, sliding in and out of her pussy, and the cum suddenly rushed to the surface. He held her down hard on his dick, and shot the contents of his balls deep inside her. "Shit, baby! Damn, I'm nutting all in this pussy!" he said as he came inside of her, releasing what felt like a gallon of cum. The way her pussy was gripping him, it almost felt like it was pulling the cum out of him.

Shila wrapped her arms around his neck and whispered, "Yes, baby. Get it all out. Get it all out," as she slowly whined her hips against him and took in every last drop of cum.

"Sheesh! Damn, get up slowly, boo. It's sensitive," he said, laughing. She leaned to the side and slid off as she held her hand under her pussy. Even as deep as he had poured his cum inside her, she could still feel a large quantity of it rushing to the surface of her pussy lips, and out onto her hand. He had came a lot, and it made her especially happy that she was able to make him cum like that. To her, it made her feel as though his body wanted her as much as her body wanted him. She put her mouth back on his dick and gently licked and sucked him clean since she didn't have anything in the car to wipe him off with.

"I usually have some wipes, but I didn't bring my purse. Sorry."

"It's all good," he said, pulling his pants up.

Shila pulled her pants up with one hand, while holding the load that had dropped out of her in the other one. After getting them most of the way up, she opened the door and flung it out on the ground.

"You was supposed to lick that off your hand."

"Damn, I didn't think about that. Next time I will."

CHAPTER
FIFTY-THREE

Steve then got back into his car and followed her to the nearest drug store. He went inside with her, and they bought a Plan B. When they got back outside, he carefully instructed her to open her mouth wide so he could see her put it in, and then he inspected her mouth carefully afterward to make sure she swallowed it. He didn't want her playing any games, and him having a baby on the way. He was terrified, but she did what she was told and he kissed her before she left.

On his way home, he started feeling guilty again. He didn't know what he wanted to do with everything, and he couldn't help but feel bad about it all. It was like he was stuck with having to keep having sex with Shila. He felt horrible for cheating on Angelia. He didn't understand how guys did it and didn't have any issues with it. He had been happy and content with one girl for the last 6-7 years, and he was fine with that. And seeing how much mental energy and time he had to spend on both of them was crazy to him. It was like Shila was stealing his sex drive away that he normally would have saved for Angelia. So far it had been fun, but he was not sure how much longer he would be able to keep this up. It was becoming risky, and especially with the amount of money that was about to start flowing in, there was no room for games. He had to get focused, and figure it out.

On the way back home, he stopped to buy a money counter. Selecting a good model that would suit his needs perfectly. When he pulled up at the house, he saw that Angelia was still out, probably cruising around and showing off her new car. He was thinking about what Shila had been saying, so he texted her.

Steve: So if I don't want to be flashy and standing out, what's a cool whip to get that's smooth? What do you think I'd look good in that wouldn't be too over the top?

Shila: It's a lot to choose from, but I can see you in a pickup truck, F-150 or something.

Steve: Ram 1500?

Shila: Yeah, those are cute too. Grown man truck, although it's a lot of lil' boys around here with them Lol.

Steve: You silly, well I'll blend right in.

Shila: True True.

Steve: Thanks.

Shila: You getting one?

Steve: Maybe one day. I don't see a need for it at the moment.

Almost immediately after replying to Shila, Steve could hear a car pulling up outside. He instantly assumed that Angelia was back, judging by the sound of the car. Unconsciously, he started smelling himself, his clothes, arms, and body, to make sure he wasn't smelling to much like a woman's perfume. He also checked his pants to see if he still had any wet stains from the head and the sex. Luckily for him, his pants were dry. He exhaled on his palms to smell his breath. To him, his breath had a slight smell of pussy. He quickly looked around for a mint or some gum. There was nothing around. He straightened up, and decided to sit still and keep his cool. Soon, Angelia came walking through the door.

"Heyyy!" she said with a big smile as she came towards him and went in for a kiss, but he dodged her and hugged her instead. She tried to kiss him again two more times, and he dodged her both times, trying his best to make sure she wouldn't smell the scent of another woman on his lips, or taste it.

"Gimme a kiss," she said, moving her head with his, trying to connect lips with him.

"Naw, I just had onions," he lied, not wanting to kiss her with pussy lips. She wasn't letting go of this one. She kept insisting on a kiss, and Steve started to think that the longer he resisted, the more likely she was going to suspect that something was wrong, and he'd only be digging his own grave. He then swallowed his own saliva in an attempt to clean his own mouth, and finally, his lips met with hers.

"I don't care, boy. I been smelling your morning breath for years," she said, pecking him on the lips again. Steve paused for a moment and hesitated, waiting for her to say something. She didn't seem to notice though, and Steve silently exhaled a sigh of relief.

"I think I'ma take off to Texas in the morning," he said as casually as possible.

"Dang, you can't wait one more day? You know I leave Friday."

"Naw, I would if I could, but I gotta be down there before Friday."

"Oh, okay. Okay, baby. Do whatever you need to do. If you gone be leaving at like 3 or 4 in the morning like last time, you might want to lay down and go to sleep early tonight."

"I know. I thought about that. I'm bouta go shower in a minute and start relaxing."

"I'll be waking you up before then," she said, smiling. She was looking good today in her tight navy blue denim jeans with a white button up collar shirt that tied in the front.

Steve looked her up and down and smiled. "Where you been, looking like that?"

"Looking like what?"

"All sexy and shit. Your booty bout to burst out them pants. God damn!"

She giggled, and ran her hand over her butt, sticking it out a little for him to get an even better view of it. "I went by my mom's, aunt's, Esha's, and Candy's house to show all of them my new car."

"You still be talking to Candy?"

"Yeah, that's my girl. I just haven't said much about her lately, that's all."

CHAPTER
FIFTY-FOUR

Steve packed his duffle bag up with some comfortable clothes, and got all of his money organized and ready. He took a hot shower while thinking through everything he wanted to get done before he laid down that evening. After putting the few things together he needed, he laid down and fell asleep.

A couple hours later, he was woken up to Angelia giving him head. He opened his eyes and looked down to see her head bobbing up and down on his shaft. He then reached over to his nightstand to grab his phone and check the time. It was 1:00 a.m., and although he was tired, he figured that he should probably just let her do what she was doing so she didn't get upset. While it continued, he ended up waking up fully, and decided to flip her over and make love to her. He laid her down with her back flat on the bed and used the night to his advantage. He watched her face in the dim light as he thrust himself inside her, stroking back and forth nice and slowly. His idea was to keep her wanting more, while at the same time making her cum over and over again. He loved making her moan and cum, and he also loved it when she'd call him Papi.

They both went at each other for what ended up being hours, and by the time they finished, it was almost 3 a.m., and he figured that he should probably just stay up. Angelia had orgasmed multiple times, and she fell asleep, completely exhausted.

Steve got up, and got dressed. He carried his stuff downstairs and went through all of it, making sure he wasn't forgetting anything. He was satisfied that he had everything he needed, so he packed his car, and stashed the money. Within the next 5 minutes, he was out the door. It was 3:40 a.m., and he felt like he was leaving at a perfect time.

The weather was decent the whole way down, but the drive was long and boring to him. The only thing that motivated him to keep driving was knowing what he was driving for. He decided that he would just stop as he felt like it to nap or stretch his legs.

He arrived in San Antonio, Texas around 4 p.m. the next day after all the stops and sleeping. He had never been to San Antonio before, but he found it to be a beautiful city. It was set up much differently than Metro Detroit, and he was excited to check out a few things while he was there but most importantly, he was ready to meet Karo. He drove straight to the address he was given, and saw the restaurant. It was packed, but he learned that it closed at 8 p.m., so he decided he was going to explore the city for a few hours and then come back.

After checking out a few different places, he drove back to the restaurant, pulling up about 7:45. The parking lot was emptying out, and he thought it would be a good time to walk inside and ask for her, so he parked and went in. There was a young lady sitting at the first table inside the door, wrapping silverware up in napkins.

"Habla Ingles?"

"Yes," she replied.

"Is Karo here today?"

"Yes, I'll go get her. One moment, I'll be right back."

Not too long after the young lady disappeared into the back, a short lady, who looked to be in her mid-40's came walking from the back. It was hard to tell the age of this woman, because she had a great body, with wide hips and a nice butt. Her skin was light, and her hair was long and pulled back in a ponytail. She had on jeans and a t-shirt that said the company name on it.

"Can I help you?"

"Yes, I'm Steve. My Uncle Swift told me I could find you here. I'm looking for work."

Karo's face changed immediately. At first, it was the face of a normal, friendly company employee, but after Steve spoke, her expression became completely straight and cold. She looked him from head to toe, scanning him with her eyes as she processed what he had just said. After about a minute, she turned around and started to walk away, but waved her hand for him to follow her. As he walked behind her toward the back, she never said a word to him again until they were in the back office with the door closed. Steve could feel a strong and intimidating aura oozing from her very being. He started to wonder how somebody who looked so relatively short and harmless a minute ago, suddenly became the scariest person in the room. Everything Uncle Swift had said about Karo, as far as he could tell, was true, and perhaps even an understatement.

CHAPTER
FIFTY-FIVE

"Wait here. Have a seat," she said as she walked out and closed the door behind her. Steve sat in the chair in the office, looking around at what appeared to be a normal office that you would see in the back of any restaurant. There were files, ordering forms, a dusty computer, and papers all over the desk. About 3 minutes later, three large Mexican men that looked like security guards came walking in wearing all black, carrying guns the size of a 7 year old child.

"Pat him down," Karo instructed coldly. One of the men pulled Steve to his feet, and held his arm while the other two looked him over, patting him down thoroughly. "Where's your cell phone?" she asked as they finished.

"In my car, center console," he replied nervously. One of the guys took his car keys, and went out and brought it back. While he was out there, he looked through his car and checked his plates.

"So Swift is your uncle?"

"Yes, ma'am."

"Don't call me ma'am," she said, still maintaining her cold, straight, expressionless face.

"Sorry, I mean, yes. He's my uncle."

"Get up. Come with me." She waved her hand for him to follow her. The two men who were still in the room followed them with guns pointed directly at his back. She brought him into a back room where there were five other Mexicans wearing ski masks gathered around a guy who was laying on the ground, struggling. The guy was covered in blood, breathing heavily while blood poured from his mouth. He was fighting for his life. His eyes were huge, and his shirt was ripped, with one of the sleeves torn all the way off. This man had no shoes or socks on, and his khaki pants looked like they were drenched in blood from wounds on his legs.

Steve's heart sank as he saw the condition of this man. He threw a quick glance at Karo, who was already looking at him, awaiting his reaction, with her stone cold eyes. He was confused, and didn't really understand exactly what was happening, but he hoped to God he wasn't about to end up dead. The man on the ground was alive, but in a bloody, horrible way. The sight of him alone caused Steve's heart to skip a beat, and sweat began to pour down his forehead. He felt like hyperventilating as his heart raced, feeling like it was about to jump out of the shirt he was wearing.

Seconds later, one of the guys wearing a ski mask took a butcher knife out and stabbed the guy in the upper right corner of his chest, then slowly dragged the knife down to his stomach, across it, and then back up to the left part of his chest, slicing a big "U" shape through his whole torso. The man couldn't even scream as the knife tore through his skin, sinking deeply into his flesh. The sound of the knife cutting through his body made Steve almost vomit. He could not believe what his eyes were seeing. The helpless guy was still alive though. His body was twitching and shaking. It looked like he wanted to say something, but nothing was coming out of his mouth, except for a steady stream of blood. After a couple seconds, the twitching and shaking stopped, but Steve could see the man still gasping for breath. The men then went back to work on him again.

They started to peel his skin back, revealing the muscle and sinews. Every organ twitched and moved with life. The guy, though he seemed not present, was flopping around on the ground with his eyes wide open. One of the men cut through his abdominal muscle to reveal his liver, and ripped a thumb-sized piece off of it and held it in the air. It dripped with blood. He looked at Karo, then Steve, then tilted his head back and dropped the piece of liver into his mouth and began to chew it.

Steve looked at Karo, then the man standing next to him, and started vomiting everything he ate earlier. All the guys were laughing as they watched this guy suffer. It seemed like it took forever for the few final movements and twitches of his body to finally come to a complete stop. Steve was breathing heavily, down on one knee with vomit on the floor in front of him, and scared out of his mind.

"Come," Karo said, and Steve got up and gladly followed her out of the room, away from the bloody execution scene. He prayed that his uncle didn't owe them anything. All kinds of thoughts ran through his head, and he even considered making a run for it. She led him back into the small office and closed the door behind them. "Sit."

He sat down, and she handed him a napkin to wipe the vomit from his goatee. "How is your uncle?" she asked with a completely new tone.

"Good," he replied, shaking his head up and down.

"Swift used to work for me for a long time, and he made me lots of money. You know that?"

"Yes."

"I never had a problem with him. He always paid on time. He kept things going for years and never got caught." She spoke in a strong accent, but Steve understood what she was saying clearly. "Well, he's caught cases over the years, but he beat them every time . . . state, Feds, don't matter. I hate that they have him for murder. You make sure to tell him when he comes home to come see me. I am going to buy him anything he wants, just to get his life back started again."

"Okay, I will."

"So, we found $100,000 stashed in your car. I'm guessing that's for me?"

"Yes, it is."

"What you want me to do with that? Wipe my pussy?"

"My uncle said it would -."

"Quiet. After the foundation your uncle has built with me, I wouldn't dare take money from him or from you, being that he sent you. Understand? Your money is no good. With that said, it will be placed back into your stash spot, which is very amateur. It's not close to good enough. I have someone in Detroit, where you will get all your stash spots built. Understand? This is not negotiable."

"Yes. Understood," he replied with a nod.

"Your uncle must really believe in you and trust you to work for me, because he know what I would do to you, him, your parents, kids, siblings, aunts, uncles, grandparents, wife, the list is endless. So, I'm going to give you a chance. I'll give you 15 kilos. Shipping and handling is included in the price, which is $30,000 each. As you know, the prices are sky high right now because of politics, of course, but it will get better soon. Is $30,000 okay? Can you handle 15 kilos?"

"Yes, that price is fine, and yes, I can handle them."

"Okay, do you have an address where you want them?" she asked, handing him a pen and a piece of paper.

Steve wrote down his mom's new address on the piece of paper.

"Okay. I'll have them dropped off Monday morning." A man then came through the office door with a cell phone and handed it to Steve. "Only text 'ready' when you are done, and need more. If the address changes, let me know. Money will be picked up and more will be dropped off, all in one transaction."

"Okay."

"Be safe. Nice to meet you, Steve," she said, extending her hand.

"Nice to meet you too. Thank you so much." He stood up, and she walked him out to his car.

When they got outside they stood outside his car, and she looked at him oddly then said, "I don't really like your name. How about S?"

"S?" he asked.

"Yeah, S. It's sexier. I'm going to call you that," she said as she walked inside and waved goodbye to him.

CHAPTER
FIFTY-SIX

As Angelia laid in the bed with Jon Jon inside their luxury master room in the AirBnB mansion he had rented for the weekend, she thought about how much fun she had at the beach and all the exclusive places Jon Jon had taken her so far. The only light in the house came from the full moon outside. Since they were flying out tomorrow evening, she didn't want to sleep, although Esha and Jon Jon's brother were both sleeping soundly. All the drinks and shots of Patron had them passed out, but Angelia wanted to stay up and enjoy every last minute. She laid there, wide awake, with her head resting on Jon Jon's chest.

"This weekend flew by too fast. We have to do this again soon. Tomorrow is already Sunday and we gotta go back," she wined, kissing him on the chin.

"We will, boo. No worries," he said, then went silent. Both of them were drunk, but Jon Jon was in deep thought.

"What's wrong?" she asked.

"I just don't understand you sometimes," he replied, adjusting himself in the bed a little.

"What you mean?" she asked as she sat up to look at him.

"You say you want to be with a nigga. We been fucking for a year now, and you still making me use a condom. I thought me bringing you out here, you would loosen up a little bit. Yesterday, we fucked four times, and every single time, you was on the condom thing, like I got something or something. Or you got something."

"No, it's not about that. I'm not worried about you having something. Well, kind of, because I don't know who else you having sex with. I don't want to catch something then give it to him, you know, then what I look like?"

"You think I will give you a STD? People know when they got shit."

"No, I don't think that. I just like to be safe."

"I'm tired of being safe. We be fucking too much for me to be using condoms. I be eating your pussy and ass. You suck my dick and eat my ass. I mean, we already going all the way. We might as well lose this condom shit," he said, slurring his words with low eyes. "You say you my baby, but you making me use a condom every single damn time. Not once have I been inside you without a condom."

Angelia was drunk, but she was still trying to think of a better reason as to why she hadn't let him have sex with her without a condom. "You love me, Jon Jon?" she finally asked, breaking the silence.

"You know I love you. How many times I den tried to get you to leave that wack ass nigga you fuck with?"

She slapped his chest. "Stop! You such a bully," she joked.

"Suck this dick," he told her as he pushed her head down towards his dick. She got right at it, sucking and licking all over his balls. He would always bring out a different side of her, and she loved it. She stroked and sucked his dick while trying to deep throat it, but couldn't. "Spit on that dick," he told her, and she complied while still stroking it quickly. "Tell me how much you love sucking my dick," he said.

"I love it so much, Papi!" she exclaimed, still stroking and sucking it.

"Turn on the lights. I want you to look me in the eyes and tell me you love sucking my dick."

His voice was so sexy to her. It was like it penetrated her body. He had such a deep, manly voice. She got up and flicked on the lights then got back on the bed and pulled his shorts and boxer briefs off and started sucking his dick again while looking him in the eyes.

"Now tell me you love sucking my dick."

"I love sucking your dick, Papi!" she said, slobbing from the mouth but still going.

"Keep looking me in the eyes," he told her since she had glanced away. "Look me in the eyes and tell me again while you sucking it like that."

"I love sucking this dick, Papi!"

"Tell me you will never leave me."

"I will never leave you, Papi," she said, now stroking with two hands as his dick was rock hard and standing straight up.

"Tell me you love me."

"I love you, Papi," she said, sucking with no hands while starting to remove her clothes. He had her hot and dripping wet, and she loved it.

"Tell me you want me inside you with no condom."

"I want you inside me . . . Papi, with no condom."

"Now get on top of me and put this dick in you. Naw, better yet, bend over," he said, getting up, and grabbing his dick and aiming it at her. He slid it in between her pussy lips. Her pussy dripped as his dick glided inside slowly.

"How that feel?" he said as he stroked her pussy.

"So good, baby. So good," she moaned.

"Tell me it feels better with no condom," he said, stroking deeper and more aggressively.

"It feels better," she said as she gripped the sheets in an attempt to prevent herself from screaming. "I'm cumming, Papi!" she screamed out, unable to hold it in as she felt him stroking even harder. "Fuck!" she yelled as her body tensed up, and the pressure caused his dick to come out, as she squirted.

"Naw, come here. Where you going?" He grabbed her waist with his good arm and pulled her back to him.

"Okay, okay, Papi," she said out of breath.

He put his dick back inside her and started fucking her roughly as she screamed, "Baby! Papi! Papi! Papi!" He stroked her as hard and fast as he could, making her pussy squirt all over him and the bed, again and again. She continued to scream while squeezing the sheets as he pounded her pussy like Steve had never done. He beat her pussy so bad, Esha came running in from all the screams, but quickly realized that her friend was okay.

Jon Jon didn't stop or show any signs of slowing down. He kept going, making her pussy squirt over five times before he finally slowed down. The bed was soaking wet, and there was no way they were going to be sleeping in it. "Here, ride this dick until I cum," he said as he laid down. She jumped right on it and started bouncing her ass. "Turn around and do exactly what you doing. I wanna see my dick in that pussy while you bouncing that ass."

She turned around and started bouncing. "Like this, Papi?" she asked.

"Just like that," he said as he watched her ass go up and down on his dick. "You gone make me cum, baby."

"You like that, Papi?"

"You gone make me cum in this pussy baby," he said, using his hand to bounce her ass faster and harder.

"Yes, Papi! All . . . in . . . it . . . Papi!" she moaned while her ass clapped against his hips.

"Oooh, shit! Ooooh, shit! Baby, I'm cumming!" he yelled as she bounced even faster. His cum squirted inside her, and she never slowed down. "Shit, baby. Slow down, slow down," he told her as he finished nutting. "God damn!" he shouted as she was slowly grinding on his dick. "You gone fuck around and get a ring."

She giggled as she felt his dick soften up and fall out of her. She then turned around and started sucking his dick again, cleaning it up. She made her way to his ass, and started licking it for about 10 minutes with his legs all the way back. Soon, he was back inside her, and they both fell asleep while she was on top of him.

The next morning, the sun was shining through the room in bright rays when Angelia opened her eyes and tried to block it with her hand. She couldn't, so she flipped over and her heart dropped when she saw Steve standing there, pointing two guns. One at Jon Jon and the other at her.

"Bitch!"

READERS DISCUSSION QUESTIONS

1. Do you know someone like Angelia?
2. Do you think Steve shoulda broke up with Angelia when he caught her having sex with Jon Jon at their house?
3. What is keeping Steve and Angelia together?
4. What's your thoughts about Uncle Swift?
5. Is James a good friend?
6. What do you think about Esha?
7. Would you forgive a person like Angelia?
8. Should Steve had followed Jon Jon and got revenge?
9. Would you listen to rumors about who your mate is sleeping with?
10. Did Angelia make up for cheating on Steve?

Lock Down Publications and Ca$h Presents assisted publishing packages.

BASIC PACKAGE $499
Editing
Cover Design
Formatting

UPGRADED PACKAGE $800
Typing
Editing
Cover Design
Formatting

ADVANCE PACKAGE $1,200
Typing
Editing
Cover Design
Formatting
Copyright registration
Proofreading
Upload book to Amazon

LDP SUPREME PACKAGE $1,500
Typing
Editing
Cover Design
Formatting
Copyright registration
Proofreading
Set up Amazon account
Upload book to Amazon
Advertise on LDP Amazon and Facebook page

***Other services available upon request. Additional charges may apply
**Lock Down Publications
P.O. Box 944
Stockbridge, GA 30281-9998
Phone # 470 303-9761**

Jibril Williams
Submission Guideline

Submit the first three chapters of your completed manuscript to ldpsubmissions@gmail.com, subject line: Your book's title. The manuscript must be in a .doc file and sent as an attachment. Document should be in Times New Roman, double spaced and in size 12 font. Also, provide your synopsis and full contact information. If sending multiple submissions, they must each be in a separate email.

Have a story but no way to send it electronically? You can still submit to LDP/Ca$h Presents. Send in the first three chapters, written or typed, of your completed manuscript to:

**LDP: Submissions Dept
Po Box 944
Stockbridge, Ga 30281**

DO NOT send original manuscript. Must be a duplicate.

Provide your synopsis and a cover letter containing your full contact information.

Thanks for considering LDP and Ca$h Presents.

NEW RELEASES

THE MURDER QUEENS 3 by MICHAEL GALLON

GORILLAZ IN THE TRENCHES 3 by SAYNOMORE

SALUTE MY SAVAGERY by FUMIYA PAYNE

SUPER GREMLIN by KING RIO

Jibril Williams
Coming Soon from Lock Down Publications/Ca$h Presents

BLOOD OF A BOSS **VI**

SHADOWS OF THE GAME II

TRAP BASTARD II

By **Askari**

LOYAL TO THE GAME **IV**

By **T.J. & Jelissa**

TRUE SAVAGE **VIII**

MIDNIGHT CARTEL IV

DOPE BOY MAGIC IV

CITY OF KINGZ III

NIGHTMARE ON SILENT AVE II

THE PLUG OF LIL MEXICO II

CLASSIC CITY II

By **Chris Green**

BLAST FOR ME **III**

A SAVAGE DOPEBOY III

CUTTHROAT MAFIA III

DUFFLE BAG CARTEL VII

HEARTLESS GOON VI

By **Ghost**

A HUSTLER'S DECEIT III

KILL ZONE II

BAE BELONGS TO ME III

TIL DEATH II

By **Aryanna**

KING OF THE TRAP III

By **T.J. Edwards**

GORILLAZ IN THE BAY V

3X KRAZY III
STRAIGHT BEAST MODE III
De'Kari
KINGPIN KILLAZ IV
STREET KINGS III
PAID IN BLOOD III
CARTEL KILLAZ IV
DOPE GODS III
Hood Rich
SINS OF A HUSTLA II
ASAD
YAYO V
Bred In The Game 2
S. Allen
THE STREETS WILL TALK II
By Yolanda Moore
SON OF A DOPE FIEND III
HEAVEN GOT A GHETTO III
SKI MASK MONEY III
By Renta
LOYALTY AIN'T PROMISED III
By Keith Williams
I'M NOTHING WITHOUT HIS LOVE II
SINS OF A THUG II
TO THE THUG I LOVED BEFORE II
IN A HUSTLER I TRUST II
By Monet Dragun
QUIET MONEY IV
EXTENDED CLIP III

Jibril Williams
THUG LIFE IV

By **Trai'Quan**
THE STREETS MADE ME IV

By **Larry D. Wright**
IF YOU CROSS ME ONCE III

ANGEL V

By **Anthony Fields**
THE STREETS WILL NEVER CLOSE IV

By **K'ajji**
HARD AND RUTHLESS III

KILLA KOUNTY IV

By **Khufu**
MONEY GAME III

By **Smoove Dolla**
JACK BOYS VS DOPE BOYS IV

A GANGSTA'S QUR'AN V

COKE GIRLZ II

COKE BOYS II

LIFE OF A SAVAGE V

CHI'RAQ GANGSTAS V

SOSA GANG III

BRONX SAVAGES II

BODYMORE KINGPINS II

BLOOD OF A GOON II

By **Romell Tukes**
MURDA WAS THE CASE III

Elijah R. Freeman
AN UNFORESEEN LOVE IV

BABY, I'M WINTERTIME COLD III

By **Meesha**

QUEEN OF THE ZOO III

By **Black Migo**

CONFESSIONS OF A JACKBOY III

By **Nicholas Lock**

KING KILLA II

By **Vincent "Vitto" Holloway**

BETRAYAL OF A THUG III

By **Fre$h**

THE BIRTH OF A GANGSTER III

By **Delmont Player**

TREAL LOVE II

By **Le'Monica Jackson**

FOR THE LOVE OF BLOOD III

By **Jamel Mitchell**

RAN OFF ON DA PLUG II

By **Paper Boi Rari**

HOOD CONSIGLIERE III

By **Keese**

PRETTY GIRLS DO NASTY THINGS II

By **Nicole Goosby**

LOVE IN THE TRENCHES II

By **Corey Robinson**

IT'S JUST ME AND YOU II

By **Ah'Million**

FOREVER GANGSTA III

By **Adrian Dulan**

THE COCAINE PRINCESS IX

Jibril Williams
SUPER GREMLIN II
By King Rio
CRIME BOSS II
Playa Ray
LOYALTY IS EVERYTHING III
Molotti
HERE TODAY GONE TOMORROW II
By Fly Rock
REAL G'S MOVE IN SILENCE II
By Von Diesel
GRIMEY WAYS IV
By Ray Vinci
SALUTE MY SAVAGERY II
By Fumiya Payne

<u>Available Now</u>

RESTRAINING ORDER **I & II**
By **CA$H & Coffee**
LOVE KNOWS NO BOUNDARIES **I II & III**
By **Coffee**
RAISED AS A GOON I, II, III & IV
BRED BY THE SLUMS I, II, III
BLAST FOR ME I & II

ROTTEN TO THE CORE I II III
A BRONX TALE I, II, III
DUFFLE BAG CARTEL I II III IV V VI
HEARTLESS GOON I II III IV V
A SAVAGE DOPEBOY I II
DRUG LORDS I II III
CUTTHROAT MAFIA I II
KING OF THE TRENCHES
By **Ghost**
LAY IT DOWN **I & II**
LAST OF A DYING BREED I II
BLOOD STAINS OF A SHOTTA I & II III
By **Jamaica**
LOYAL TO THE GAME I II III
LIFE OF SIN I, II III
By **TJ & Jelissa**
BLOODY COMMAS I & II
SKI MASK CARTEL I II & III
KING OF NEW YORK I II,III IV V
RISE TO POWER I II III
COKE KINGS I II III IV V
BORN HEARTLESS I II III IV
KING OF THE TRAP I II
By **T.J. Edwards**
IF LOVING HIM IS WRONG…I & II
LOVE ME EVEN WHEN IT HURTS I II III
By **Jelissa**
WHEN THE STREETS CLAP BACK I & II III
THE HEART OF A SAVAGE I II III IV

Jibril Williams
MONEY MAFIA I II
LOYAL TO THE SOIL I II III

By **Jibril Williams**
A DISTINGUISHED THUG STOLE MY HEART I II & III
LOVE SHOULDN'T HURT I II III IV
RENEGADE BOYS I II III IV
PAID IN KARMA I II III
SAVAGE STORMS I II III
AN UNFORESEEN LOVE I II III
BABY, I'M WINTERTIME COLD I II

By **Meesha**
A GANGSTER'S CODE I &, II III
A GANGSTER'S SYN I II III
THE SAVAGE LIFE I II III
CHAINED TO THE STREETS I II III
BLOOD ON THE MONEY I II III
A GANGSTA'S PAIN I II III

By **J-Blunt**
PUSH IT TO THE LIMIT

By **Bre' Hayes**
BLOOD OF A BOSS **I, II, III, IV, V**
SHADOWS OF THE GAME
TRAP BASTARD

By **Askari**
THE STREETS BLEED MURDER **I, II & III**
THE HEART OF A GANGSTA I II& III

By **Jerry Jackson**
CUM FOR ME I II III IV V VI VII VIII

An **LDP Erotica Collaboration**

BRIDE OF A HUSTLA **I II & II**

THE FETTI GIRLS **I, II& III**

CORRUPTED BY A GANGSTA I, II III, IV

BLINDED BY HIS LOVE

THE PRICE YOU PAY FOR LOVE I, II ,III

DOPE GIRL MAGIC I II III

By **Destiny Skai**

WHEN A GOOD GIRL GOES BAD

By **Adrienne**

THE COST OF LOYALTY I II III

By **Kweli**

A GANGSTER'S REVENGE **I II III & IV**

THE BOSS MAN'S DAUGHTERS I II III IV V

A SAVAGE LOVE **I & II**

BAE BELONGS TO ME I II

A HUSTLER'S DECEIT I, II, III

WHAT BAD BITCHES DO I, II, III

SOUL OF A MONSTER I II III

KILL ZONE

A DOPE BOY'S QUEEN I II III

TIL DEATH

By **Aryanna**

A KINGPIN'S AMBITON

A KINGPIN'S AMBITION **II**

I MURDER FOR THE DOUGH

By **Ambitious**

TRUE SAVAGE I II III IV V VI VII

DOPE BOY MAGIC I, II, III

MIDNIGHT CARTEL I II III

By **Jibril Williams**
CITY OF KINGZ I II
NIGHTMARE ON SILENT AVE
THE PLUG OF LIL MEXICO II
CLASSIC CITY

By **Chris Green**
A DOPEBOY'S PRAYER

By **Eddie "Wolf" Lee**
THE KING CARTEL **I, II & III**

By **Frank Gresham**
THESE NIGGAS AIN'T LOYAL **I, II & III**

By **Nikki Tee**
GANGSTA SHYT **I II &III**

By **CATO**
THE ULTIMATE BETRAYAL

By **Phoenix**
BOSS'N UP **I , II & III**

By **Royal Nicole**
I LOVE YOU TO DEATH

By **Destiny J**
I RIDE FOR MY HITTA
I STILL RIDE FOR MY HITTA

By **Misty Holt**
LOVE & CHASIN' PAPER

By **Qay Crockett**
TO DIE IN VAIN
SINS OF A HUSTLA

By **ASAD**
BROOKLYN HUSTLAZ

By **Boogsy Morina**

BROOKLYN ON LOCK I & II
By **Sonovia**
GANGSTA CITY
By **Teddy Duke**
A DRUG KING AND HIS DIAMOND I & II III
A DOPEMAN'S RICHES
HER MAN, MINE'S TOO I, II
CASH MONEY HO'S
THE WIFEY I USED TO BE I II
PRETTY GIRLS DO NASTY THINGS
By **Nicole Goosby**
TRAPHOUSE KING **I II & III**
KINGPIN KILLAZ I II III
STREET KINGS I II
PAID IN BLOOD **I II**
CARTEL KILLAZ I II III
DOPE GODS I II
By **Hood Rich**
LIPSTICK KILLAH **I, II, III**
CRIME OF PASSION I II & III
FRIEND OR FOE I II III
By **Mimi**
STEADY MOBBN' **I, II, III**
THE STREETS STAINED MY SOUL I II III
By **Marcellus Allen**
WHO SHOT YA **I, II, III**
SON OF A DOPE FIEND I II
HEAVEN GOT A GHETTO I II
SKI MASK MONEY I II

Jibril Williams
Renta
GORILLAZ IN THE BAY **I II III IV**
TEARS OF A GANGSTA I II
3X KRAZY I II
STRAIGHT BEAST MODE I II
DE'KARI
TRIGGADALE I II III
MURDAROBER WAS THE CASE I II
Elijah R. Freeman
GOD BLESS THE TRAPPERS I, II, III
THESE SCANDALOUS STREETS I, II, III
FEAR MY GANGSTA I, II, III IV, V
THESE STREETS DON'T LOVE NOBODY I, II
BURY ME A G I, II, III, IV, V
A GANGSTA'S EMPIRE I, II, III, IV
THE DOPEMAN'S BODYGAURD I II
THE REALEST KILLAZ I II III
THE LAST OF THE OGS I II III
Tranay Adams
THE STREETS ARE CALLING
Duquie Wilson
MARRIED TO A BOSS I II III
By Destiny Skai & Chris Green
KINGZ OF THE GAME I II III IV V VI VII
CRIME BOSS
Playa Ray
SLAUGHTER GANG I II III
RUTHLESS HEART I II III
By Willie Slaughter

FUK SHYT
By Blakk Diamond
DON'T F#CK WITH MY HEART I II
By Linnea
ADDICTED TO THE DRAMA I II III
IN THE ARM OF HIS BOSS II
By Jamila
YAYO I II III IV
A SHOOTER'S AMBITION I II
BRED IN THE GAME
By S. Allen
TRAP GOD I II III
RICH $AVAGE I II III
MONEY IN THE GRAVE I II III
By Martell Troublesome Bolden
FOREVER GANGSTA I II
GLOCKS ON SATIN SHEETS I II
By Adrian Dulan
TOE TAGZ I II III IV
LEVELS TO THIS SHYT I II
IT'S JUST ME AND YOU
By Ah'Million
KINGPIN DREAMS I II III
RAN OFF ON DA PLUG
By Paper Boi Rari
CONFESSIONS OF A GANGSTA I II III IV
CONFESSIONS OF A JACKBOY I II
By Nicholas Lock
I'M NOTHING WITHOUT HIS LOVE

Jibril Williams
SINS OF A THUG
TO THE THUG I LOVED BEFORE
A GANGSTA SAVED XMAS
IN A HUSTLER I TRUST
By Monet Dragun
CAUGHT UP IN THE LIFE I II III
THE STREETS NEVER LET GO I II III
By Robert Baptiste
NEW TO THE GAME I II III
MONEY, MURDER & MEMORIES I II III
By **Malik D. Rice**
LIFE OF A SAVAGE I II III IV
A GANGSTA'S QUR'AN I II III IV
MURDA SEASON I II III
GANGLAND CARTEL I II III
CHI'RAQ GANGSTAS I II III IV
KILLERS ON ELM STREET I II III
JACK BOYZ N DA BRONX I II III
A DOPEBOY'S DREAM I II III
JACK BOYS VS DOPE BOYS I II III
COKE GIRLZ
COKE BOYS
SOSA GANG I II
BRONX SAVAGES
BODYMORE KINGPINS
BLOOD OF A GOON
By Romell Tukes
LOYALTY AIN'T PROMISED I II
By Keith Williams

QUIET MONEY I II III
THUG LIFE I II III
EXTENDED CLIP I II
A GANGSTA'S PARADISE
By **Trai'Quan**
THE STREETS MADE ME I II III
By **Larry D. Wright**
THE ULTIMATE SACRIFICE I, II, III, IV, V, VI
KHADIFI
IF YOU CROSS ME ONCE I II
ANGEL I II III IV
IN THE BLINK OF AN EYE
By **Anthony Fields**
THE LIFE OF A HOOD STAR
By **Ca$h & Rashia Wilson**
THE STREETS WILL NEVER CLOSE I II III
By **K'ajji**
CREAM I II III
THE STREETS WILL TALK
By **Yolanda Moore**
NIGHTMARES OF A HUSTLA I II III
By **King Dream**
CONCRETE KILLA I II III
VICIOUS LOYALTY I II III
By **Kingpen**
HARD AND RUTHLESS I II
MOB TOWN 251
THE BILLIONAIRE BENTLEYS I II III
REAL G'S MOVE IN SILENCE

Jibril Williams
By Von Diesel
GHOST MOB
Stilloan Robinson
MOB TIES I II III IV V VI
SOUL OF A HUSTLER, HEART OF A KILLER I II
GORILLAZ IN THE TRENCHES I II III
By SayNoMore
BODYMORE MURDERLAND I II III
THE BIRTH OF A GANGSTER I II
By Delmont Player
FOR THE LOVE OF A BOSS
By C. D. Blue
MOBBED UP I II III IV
THE BRICK MAN I II III IV V
THE COCAINE PRINCESS I II III IV V VI VII VIII
SUPER GREMLIN
By King Rio
KILLA KOUNTY I II III IV
By Khufu
MONEY GAME I II
By Smoove Dolla
A GANGSTA'S KARMA I II III
By FLAME
KING OF THE TRENCHES I II III
by **GHOST & TRANAY ADAMS**
QUEEN OF THE ZOO I II
By **Black Migo**
GRIMEY WAYS I II III
By Ray Vinci

XMAS WITH AN ATL SHOOTER
By Ca$h & Destiny Skai
KING KILLA
By Vincent "Vitto" Holloway
BETRAYAL OF A THUG I II
By Fre$h
THE MURDER QUEENS I II III
By Michael Gallon
TREAL LOVE
By Le'Monica Jackson
FOR THE LOVE OF BLOOD I II
By Jamel Mitchell
HOOD CONSIGLIERE I II
By Keese
PROTÉGÉ OF A LEGEND I II III
LOVE IN THE TRENCHES
By Corey Robinson
BORN IN THE GRAVE I II III
By Self Made Tay
MOAN IN MY MOUTH
By XTASY
TORN BETWEEN A GANGSTER AND A GENTLEMAN
By J-BLUNT & Miss Kim
LOYALTY IS EVERYTHING I II
Molotti
HERE TODAY GONE TOMORROW
By Fly Rock
PILLOW PRINCESS
By S. Hawkins

Jibril Williams
NAÏVE TO THE STREETS

WOMEN LIE MEN LIE I II III

GIRLS FALL LIKE DOMINOS

STACK BEFORE YOU SPURLGE

FIFTY SHADES OF SNOW I II III

By A. Roy Milligan
SALUTE MY SAVAGERY

By Fumiya Payne

BOOKS BY LDP'S CEO, CA$H

TRUST IN NO MAN
TRUST IN NO MAN 2
TRUST IN NO MAN 3
BONDED BY BLOOD
SHORTY GOT A THUG
THUGS CRY
THUGS CRY 2
THUGS CRY 3
TRUST NO BITCH
TRUST NO BITCH 2
TRUST NO BITCH 3
TIL MY CASKET DROPS
RESTRAINING ORDER
RESTRAINING ORDER 2
IN LOVE WITH A CONVICT
LIFE OF A HOOD STAR
XMAS WITH AN ATL SHOOTER

Jibril Williams